# THE SEARCH FOR SARA SANDERSON

*Other Avon Camelot Books by*
**Thomas McKean**

THE ANTI-PEGGY PLOT
MOROCCAN MYSTERY
VAMPIRE VACATION

Born in New York, THOMAS MCKEAN has lived and worked in various parts of the United States, Europe, and North Africa. Among his occupations, he has been a waiter, teacher, artist, storyteller, and writer and director of children's theatre. He resides in New York City. THE SEARCH FOR SARA SANDERSON is the author's fourth Avon Camelot book for young readers.

# THE SEARCH FOR SARA SANDERSON

Written and Illustrated by

## Thomas McKean

THE SANDERSONS
Sara • Sartorius • Sigmund • Sidney • Sassafras

AN AVON CAMELOT BOOK

THE SEARCH FOR SARA SANDERSON is an original publication of Avon Books. This work has never before appeared in book form.


AVON BOOKS
A division of
The Hearst Corporation
105 Madison Avenue
New York, New York 10016

Text and illustrations copyright © 1987 by Thomas McKean
Published by arrangement with the author
Library of Congress Catalog Card Number: 87-1059
ISBN: 0-380-75295-6
RL: 4.7

**Library of Congress Cataloging in Publication Data:**

McKean, Thomas.
  The search for Sara Sanderson.

  (An Avon Camelot book)
  Summary: When Leo, Beth, and Teasdale decide to find their father a wife for his birthday present, they become involved in a dangerous search for a real missing heiress.
  [1. Mystery and detective stories]  I. Title.
PZ7.M478658Se      1987      [Fic]        87-1059

First Camelot Printing: August 1987

CAMELOT TRADEMARK REG. U.S. PAT. OFF. AND IN OTHER COUNTRIES, MARCA REGISTRADA, HECHO EN U.S.A.

Printed in the U.S.A.

OPM   10  9  8  7  6  5  4  3  2  1

For
Connie and Andy,
Fern Else,
and
Evan Thomas McKean

with great thanks
to
Ellen Krieger

# Table of Contents

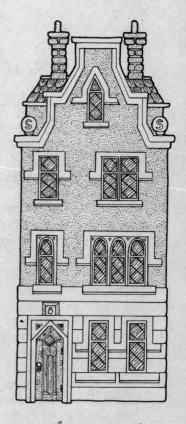

*The Home of*
SARA SANDERSON
242 East 78th Street
New York, New York

*The Home of*
SIDNEY SANDERSON
8 Gramercy Park South
New York, New York

The Home of
SASSAFRAS SANDERSON
19 Perry Street
New York, New York

The Home of
SARTORIUS SANDERSON
196 West 89th Street
New York, New York

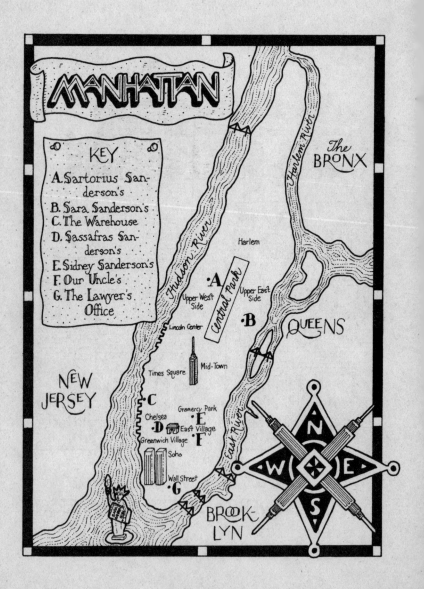

# THE SEARCH FOR
# SARA SANDERSON

# Chapter One

# August 5th—
# Afternoon & Evening

For our dad's forty-second birthday we decided to give him a wife. We decided this on August 5th, which gave us only ten days, since our dad's birthday was coming up on August 15th. Luckily for us, our dad was out of town on business until then. We kids were staying with our dad's brother John in his apartment in New York City. We figured New York City had to be the perfect place to find our dad a new wife—the only question was where.

"Christopher Columbus!" exclaimed Beth. "I've got it! Let's go to the next Mets game and find someone there!" Beth, who's twelve, is a big sports fan.

"No way!" countered Leo. "Our dad doesn't like baseball. I say we go to the planetarium and find him an expert on outer space." Leo, who's nine and the baby of the family, is the world's greatest UFO enthusiast.

"Don't be so dumb, Leo," said Beth, shaking her head. "Our dad doesn't care about outer space, ei-

1

ther." She then paused and said, "How about you, Teasdale—any bright ideas?"

Teasdale bowed his head in thought before responding. This wasn't unusual: Teasdale, who's ten, is a very thoughtful person. He's also a poet, which means he usually speaks in rhyme, even when it drives everyone around him crazy. (Here I have to add that it's one of the three kids I just mentioned who's telling this story, but I won't say which. You're going to have to guess.)

"Yes—I have a woman in mind," Teasdale finally answered, "who's thoughtful, pretty, and seems very kind."

"Who is she?" Beth and Leo asked in unison.

Teasdale cleared his throat and said:

"I went to buy some socks at the store
And she sold them to me. And what's more
I couldn't help but look and see
She was reading a book of poetry."

Even though our dad isn't exactly wild about poetry, our mom had been. And since she and our dad had been so happy together until she died a few years ago, we thought a second poetry-loving wife might be a good idea.

"But how can we all meet her?" Beth wondered. "We've got to be sure Leo and I like her too."

"Let's just go to the store where she works," suggested Leo.

"No," replied Beth. "We've got to spend a lot of time with her to size her up, and we couldn't do that in a busy store. What we have to do is get her to come here, to our uncle's apartment—and when he's out, so he won't know what we're doing."

"Hey," said Leo, "Uncle John'll be out all this afternoon."

"That's right," agreed Beth. Our uncle was in the middle of a big fight with his landlord about a wall he'd knocked down, and he'd finally gotten an appointment to meet with "The Cobra," which is what he always called the landlord.

"So how do we get her here?" wondered Leo.

"I've got an idea," said Beth, making a quick phone call to the department store. "This is the owner of the store," she said in her most grown-up and dignified voice once she'd been put through to the saleslady in the socks department. "I am *shocked,* I am absolutely *appalled* that you could sell a poor innocent child like my grandson such ill-fitting socks. If you value your job, you'll come up here to our apartment immediately to take back the merchandise!"

After she'd hung up, Beth felt awful about being so mean to the woman we wanted to marry our father. "Christopher Columbus!" she exclaimed. "She was so scared she sounded really weird on the phone. We'll have to make it up to her by being especially nice to her when she gets here."

"Good idea," Leo agreed. "Why don't we blast off to the supermarket so we can serve her a spectacular snack?"

We decided to leave Teasdale behind in case the socks lady arrived before we got back. He said he'd rather stay home and compose a sonnet to our new stepmother.

\*    \*    \*

A horrible sight awaited us upon our return.

"Christopher Columbus!" Beth exclaimed. "She doesn't look thoughtful, sweet, and kind."

"I think she looks more like a Martian invader!" gasped Leo, dropping a bag of cookies as he stared.

Teasdale didn't look too happy either; he had turned pale and was trembling slightly. In fact, he looked just about ready to faint, something he does when he's frightened or nervous.

All three of us stood and stared at the socks saleslady. She was close to six feet tall and had long gangly arms and the largest behind any of us had ever seen. Her mean-looking squinty eyes were magnified by a pair of pointy glasses, and her narrow mouth was firmly drawn into a thin angry line. She had one large hand on her left hip, while with her other she was gesticulating madly. It was hard to believe she had been Teasdale's idea of a perfect wife for our dad.

"What a sight!" she was shrieking. "What a disgrace! What a crime! Never have I seen such a shocking mess!"

We assumed she was talking about the socks Teasdale had said he'd wanted to return. Since he'd been wearing them steadily from the time he'd bought them, they *were* a bit worse for wear.

"Listen," said Beth, "you don't have to take—"

"You are absolutely correct," interrupted the socks saleslady. "I simply cannot take it a second longer! Never have I seen such filth, never have I smelled such a horrid odor!"

We now assumed she was talking about Teasdale's feet.

"Hold on a second," said Beth in a firm voice.

"Teasdale has very nice feet. They don't smell *that* bad!"

"I'm sure I don't know what you're talking about," sniffed the socks lady.

"And *I* don't know what you're talking about, either," Beth replied.

"I am talking about the state of this apartment," explained the socks lady. "It looks like a dirt bomb has exploded inside it. And," she continued, squinting at the three of us in turn, "you children look equally dirty. When was the last time you bathed?"

"Some time last week," blurted out Leo.

"I thought as much!" the socks lady gasped. "Something must be done about this," she told us, "and I am the one to do it."

She grabbed a rag from her handbag, sprayed it with disinfectant, and started cleaning the coffee table, all the while muttering to herself, "Clean and bright, clean and bright! We must make it clean and bright!" When she'd finished the coffee table, she produced a new rag from her pocketbook, sprayed it with disinfectant, and started cleaning Teasdale!

The shock of being wiped clean by this giant, angry creature finally caused Teasdale to speak for the first time since Beth and Leo had returned.

"It's the wrong socks lady!" he cried. "Get rid of her quick before she cleans us to death!"

Beth and Leo sprang into action, and after a slight scuffle, we were able to wrestle the rag from the socks lady's hand and free Teasdale from her grasp.

"I'm afraid you have to leave," announced Beth. "You are not the one we meant to invite."

"That doesn't concern me," replied the socks lady.

5

"I can see I am needed here and I plan to stay. Never before has June Sinknot fled in the face of filth! I shall remain firmly rooted to the floor until your mother returns."

Nobody felt like telling this Sinknot creature our mother was dead. There are some things too personal to tell a stranger.

"We live with our dad—" began Beth.

"Than I shall remain in this pigsty until your father returns," announced Miss Sinknot, "and when he does I shall instruct him concerning the proper method of cleaning both apartments and children."

"This isn't our dad's apartment," Leo started to explain.

June Sinknot gasped and said, "You mean you children live here alone?"

"No, it's our uncle's apartment," Beth replied.

"Then I shall stay here until your uncle arrives," vowed Miss Sinknot. "Wild horses could not drag me away. Never could I forgive myself if I were to abandon you youngsters to such a slovenly environment."

Now we were in big trouble. We had to get rid of Miss Sinknot somehow—and before our Uncle John returned from his appointment with his landlord.

Without stopping to think, Beth began, "I'm sorry, Miss Sinknot, but there's no use waiting for our uncle."

"Whyever not?" Miss Sinknot wanted to know.

"Why not?" Beth said. "Um, because he's, um . . . he's—"

"Lost in the jungle!" cried Leo suddenly.

7

"Lost in the jungle?" gasped Miss Sinknot, Beth, and Teasdale.

"That's what I said, lost in the jungle," repeated Leo. Beth remembered Leo was reading a science fiction book called *Giants from Jupiter in the Jungles of Brazil*.

"That's right," Beth went on. "Our uncle's an explorer and he's been missing in the jungle for three years. No one knows when he's coming back—if ever. That's why we're here; we drop by his apartment to water his plants. No one really lives here— that's why it's such a mess."

"Lost in the jungle," murmured Miss Sinknot. "How perfectly dreadful!"

"And that's not all!" cried Leo, who never knows when to stop. "He's been trapped by a giant cobra who'll eat him if he attempts to escape! This wicked cobra is the Lord of the Land down there!"

"Now *this* I do not believe," said Miss Sinknot firmly. "I see you are merely trying to get rid of me."

"But it's true!" we insisted.

"Nonsense!" snorted Miss Sinknot. "Being so filthy has affected your reasoning. If your uncle were indeed the prisoner of a snake, how would you know?"

"How would we know?" pondered Leo. "Um . . . um . . ."

"Simple," interjected Beth. "Once a year our uncle is allowed to telephone. But since we haven't heard from him for a long time, he can't be coming back any time soon. So there really would be no use in waiting."

June Sinknot obviously wasn't taken in by our

8

story. "I plan to stay in this apartment until your uncle's return and then we shall all clean and sanitize it together," she said.

"But—" we began.

"There can be no 'buts' about it!" said Miss Sinknot in a final tone. "I have never heard such a preposterous tale. I shall have to inform your uncle that in addition to being unclean you are untruthful."

Just then the door opened, and in stepped our Uncle John. It was a warm day, and he was wiping the sweat from his forehead. He didn't look especially neat or clean, and we were sure Miss Sinknot would dart over and start cleaning him, too.

"Hey, kids," he said. "Sorry to be late—but I had a rough trip. It's a jungle out there!"

"Did you say 'jungle'?" inquired Miss Sinknot, her voice trembling somewhat.

"That's right," our uncle answered, nodding his head politely in Miss Sinknot's direction. Not being the kind of grown-up who's always asking questions, he must have just assumed Miss Sinknot was a friend of ours—not that any of *us* would ever have a friend like *her*.

"Yes," he repeated, fanning himself with his hand, "it's a jungle out there! I feel as though I've been gone at least three years."

"Three years!" said a shaken Miss Sinknot. "You've really been gone three years?"

Uncle John must have figured Miss Sinknot was joking. "I suppose I should have telephoned—but I just wasn't able to," he responded with a grin.

"Telephoned!" gasped Miss Sinknot, inching toward the door. "Telephoned . . . jungle . . ." she repeated, half under her breath, gazing intently at our uncle's sweat-streaked face. "Then your niece and nephews weren't lying!"

"Lying?" said our uncle, quite confused. "Lying about what?"

"Lying about the Lord of the Land and—"

"Why should they lie about my landlord?" wondered our uncle, who must have misheard Miss Sinknot.

"But—but—" Miss Sinknot said. "But is he really a—really a—"

"A snake?" chuckled our uncle. "Yeah—he's a real snake, always grabbing what isn't his and trying to swallow it whole. But what can you expect? I *said* it's a jungle out there!"

"Oh my word!" shrieked Miss Sinknot, lunging toward the door. "Just imagine how filthy a snake's lair in the jungle must be! Who knows what germs lurk there!" Looking at our uncle in horror, she shrieked again and cried, "I'm getting out of here!"

Saying this, she made an insane dash for the door and disappeared down the steps like a madwoman, leaving behind the collection of socks samples she'd brought with her.

"Who was *she?*" our uncle wanted to know.

"Oh, just a door-to-door socks salesperson," explained Beth nonchalantly.

"Hmmm," said our uncle, "that's an odd career. I guess she doesn't do too well at it. Perhaps that's why she was a bit peculiar."

Later that night, while we were sitting on the sofa and comforting Teasdale, who was still upset over

**10**

being sanitized by Miss Sinknot, a can of something came sailing through the window.

It turned out to be a can of Lysol, and attached to it was a note. It read:

Dear Children,

Even though your uncle is a germ-carrying jungle-faring lunatic—and sloppy to boot—I am ashamed to have fled, leaving you children defenseless against whatever germs he was carrying in his filthy state. Rest assured I shall make it up to you.

Sincerely,<br>June Sinknot

"Christopher Columbus!" groaned Beth. "Something tells me we haven't seen the last of her."

MISS SINKNOT No. 1

# Chapter Two

# August 6th—Morning

The next day, Teasdale wanted to go to the store and locate the real socks saleslady, but Beth and Leo refused.

"We might run into Miss Sinknot again," warned Leo.

"And besides," said Beth, "who even knows if our dad would like the woman you saw? I say we better rethink this whole business."

While we were busy rethinking, the telephone rang. It turned out to be our dad. He phoned almost every other day. He said it was because he missed us, but we wondered if perhaps he was calling to make sure we were keeping out of trouble. We seem to get into trouble very easily.

"I'm curious, Dad," said Beth, trying to sound casual, "if you had to describe the perfect wife— what would she be like?"

"Oh, Beth," laughed our dad. "There's no such thing as a perfect wife—"

"But let's say there were," Beth interrupted. "Tell me what she'd be like."

Our dad paused a moment, sighed, and then answered. "Well," he said slowly, "she'd have to be intelligent, kind, and like children."

"So far, so good," said Beth, quickly writing down what our dad had said. "What else? What would she do?"

"I wouldn't really care," our dad replied, "just as long as it was work she enjoyed and found interesting."

"Okay. What would she look like?"

"Honestly, Beth," said our Dad, "how a woman looks isn't what really matters."

"I know that," Beth replied—"but if you *had* to describe your ideal wife . . ."

"Well," said our dad, "I suppose my idea of the perfect wife would be a woman around five-eight, blue eyes, blonde hair, around thirty-five or so."

"Thanks, Dad," Beth replied.

"Now," continued our Dad, "You and the boys be good! And I'll see you on the fifteenth."

"Right, Dad. And something tells me that this year you're going to get the best birthday present ever!"


"So how does this information help us?" Leo wanted to know. "Are we going to wait on the corner until a tall thirty-five-year-old blonde woman with blue eyes just happens to stroll by? How will we even know if she's married or single?"

"We'll ask her," replied Beth. "And if she isn't married, we'll ask her if she wants to be."

"This could take forever," moaned Leo. "I think locating a UFO would be easier."

"Let's not stand here complaining and cursin'," Teasdale said, "let's go find this missing person!"

**14**

"Missing person!" exclaimed Beth. "That's it!"

"That's what?" wondered Leo.

"You'll see," Beth replied. "C'mon, boys—we're off!"

Twenty minutes later we were standing outside the nearest police station, a large modern building not far from our uncle's apartment. Teasdale, who's frightened of policemen, was looking ready to faint, so Beth quickly explained why we were there.

"Listen," she said, "as Leo pointed out, finding this woman for our dad could take forever, right? So instead of doing it ourselves, we'll have the police do it for us."

"I don't think the police are in the business of finding wives," countered Leo.

"Perhaps not," agreed Beth. "But if we go to the Missing Persons Bureau and report this woman as missing, then they'll have to search for her. And when they find her, they'll tell us and we can go meet her. And if we like her, we'll introduce her to our dad."

"The plan makes sense—I can't deny it," pronounced Teasdale, "so let's just go ahead and try it."

"How may I help you?" asked a grumpy officer at the Missing Persons Bureau.

"We want to report a missing person," Beth answered.

"Well, you've come to the right place," the officer replied. "The procedure is that I ask you a few questions about the missing person and then enter the information into the computer. The computer then

**15**

compares the information entered with the information already in its memory bank, just in case someone else has reported the same person as missing.''

''I know all this kind of stuff,'' interrupted Leo. ''I'm a computer expert.''

''Isn't that nice,'' yawned the policeman. His name, he'd told us, was Joe Wypikowski. ''Now—about that missing person: What's the name?''

''Her name?'' repeated Beth. Somehow we hadn't thought to make up a name for our ''missing person.''

''Yeah,'' replied the policeman. ''What's her name?''

''We don't know!'' blurted out Leo. Our dad often says people with red hair like Leo talk too much, and I'm beginning to think he's right.

''Whaddaya mean you don't know?'' mocked the policeman. ''Why would you be looking for someone whose name you don't even know?''

''So when we find her we can ask her what it is,'' volunteered Teasdale. ''Maybe it's Shirley, maybe it's Liz.''

''Wait just a minute,'' protested the policeman. ''I can't file a report if you don't even know this person's name. Is this some kind of a prank?''

''Oh no!'' Beth said, opening her eyes wide and trying to look honest. ''Not at all! What we meant was we weren't sure what name she was using *now*— you see, she sometimes uses aliases, so we thought if we gave you a name, it might not be the one she's using at the moment.''

''All right,'' yawned the policeman, still looking tired and disinterested. ''Now for the second ques-

16

tion," he continued as he typed our answer to the first into the computer. "Can you provide a description?"

"Yup," said Beth. "She's thirty-five years old, blonde, with blue eyes, and five foot eight. She enjoys her career and likes children."

"Thirty-five, blonde, blue-eyed, female, five-eight," murmured the policeman, entering the information into the computer. "Okay," he said when he was done, "how long has this person been missing?"

"How long has she been missing?" repeated Beth, aghast. It hadn't occurred to us we'd be asked such complicated questions.

"That's what I said, how long has she been missing?"

"Forever!" said Leo in a loud voice.

"Forever?" said the policeman. "How can someone be missing forever?"

"He just means it seems like forever," Beth put in quickly. "Actually, she's been missing, um . . . oh, let's see . . ."

"Yes?" wondered the policeman.

"Three years," said Leo.

"Fine," sighed the policeman, looking somewhat bored. "And where was she last seen?" he demanded.

"Cape Canaveral," replied Leo, still hoping to find a mother interested in space travel.

"London," replied Teasdale, who's an Anglophile.

"New York City," replied Beth, trying to be practical.

"What the—" began the policeman while Beth quickly signaled to her brothers to be silent.

"What we meant was that after a trip to England she stopped in at Cape Canaveral for the afternoon

**17**

before returning to New York and then she was never seen again," explained Beth.

"Last seen—New York City," typed in the policeman with a small yawn. "Okay," he continued, "that's it for my questions. Let's see what the computer comes up with."

While we waited, the computer made lots of low humming noises and finally produced a readout. The policeman took the readout from the computer and started to read.

"Yes," he began, skimming the paper, "we do have an extensive report on the woman you described."

"But—that means someone else has reported her missing!" cried Beth.

"That's right," agreed the policeman, beginning to look less sleepy. "This dame's been reported missing by three other individuals. They said it was vital to find her . . . and . . ."

Suddenly the policeman looked very alert and not very friendly. "Holy cow!" he said. "It's her!" He folded the printout in half and threw it in the wastepaper basket behind him. Then he sat up stiffly and said, "That's all I can tell you. You have to leave now. If we can be of further assistance we'll contact you. Don't call us. Good-bye."

"But you don't even know our phone number—" we began when the policeman signaled to a guard by the door, who forcibly ejected us from the police station!

"You're not being very polite!" cried Teasdale as we were pushed out the front door of the station by a burly guard. "I'm a taxpayer and I demand to be treated right!"

18

"You're not a taxpayer," sneered the guard, "you're just a kid."

And he slammed the door behind us.

"There is something very weird going on around here," announced Beth five minutes later as we sat sipping lemonade in our favorite luncheonette. "I say we've stumbled onto a mystery, and I say we get to the bottom of it."

"But what about finding our dad a wife?" wondered Leo, who stopped blowing bubbles into his lemonade with a straw only long enough to speak.

"Listen," Beth replied, "this woman must be pretty unusual if three other people are looking for her. Someone *that* unusual might just be the perfect mother for us. We've got to find out what's going on—and that means finding out what else was on that printout!"

"Roger!" agreed Leo.

"How about you, Teasdale?" asked Beth. "Are you up for some sleuthing?"

Teasdale sighed and said:

"Sure—I guess it's our fate
Always to investigate!"

So we ordered three more lemonades and began discussing our next move.

# Chapter Three

# August 6th—Evening (from the diary of Fudge Ferrara)

It's been a busy day. I got a call this afternoon from the Boss, who said Joe down at the police station had just phoned. Joe told the Boss that three weird kids came nosing around, looking for her too. I wonder what they want with her. Joe says they seem to know a lot about her. This could mean trouble. We've got to find her before anybody else does or everything'll be ruined. Maybe those kids know something that'll help us find her.

The Boss wants me to follow the little creeps. I don't know much about kids, but I don't think I like them. I know I'm not gonna like these three. Joe says they're all strange and that one talks in rhyme. I hope we find her soon so I don't have to follow them long.

The Boss says if we find her soon I'll get something extra. I wonder where she is. I wonder if she knows what's going on.

Now I better go to bed. The Boss says I should get a lot of rest if I want to keep up with these three kids. According to Joe they move pretty fast. But no kids can outdo me!

# Chapter Four

# August 7th—Morning

None of us really wanted to go back to the police station, but we knew we had to. We arrived early in the morning, hoping that perhaps the policeman we'd seen the day before wouldn't be there yet and we'd get someone nicer. But no luck.

"I thought I told you kids to go away and stay away!" yelled the same grouchy policeman. "Now get outta here and don't come back!"

Once again we were ejected from the station.

"This whole thing is giving me the creeps," said Beth.

"What do you mean?" Leo wanted to know.

"I mean I just know somebody's up to no good. Policemen are supposed to be friendly to kids, not yell at them. Besides, ever since we left our uncle's this morning, I've had the feeling we've been followed."

All three of us looked around anxiously.

"So—what do we do now?" demanded Leo.

"I don't know about you, but I'm going to eat a banana or two," announced Teasdale, reaching into his bag and producing a banana. Teasdale claimed investigating mysteries was such exhausting work that he had to eat a bunch of bananas a day to keep his strength up.

While Teasdale ate we thought, but our thoughts were interrupted by a loud shriek from behind us.

"Clean and bright! Clean and bright! We must make it clean and bright!" cried a grating voice, and there stood June Sinknot, busily spraying a No Parking sign with Lysol. The next thing we knew, she'd darted up to us. With one quick motion, she dipped her large hand into Teasdale's bag, grabbed the banana peel he'd put in it, and threw it over her shoulder.

"One mustn't keep such dirty nasty things in a bag," she informed us, dabbing at some dirt on Leo's neck.

We were about to run when an excellent idea occurred to Beth.

"Oh, Miss Sinknot," she said, "you're just the person we were hoping to see."

"I am?" cried Miss Sinknot.

"She is?" cried Teasdale and Leo.

"Absolutely!" continued Beth. "We're in trouble deep and you can help us."

"Does something need cleaning?" inquired Miss Sinknot, dusting some invisible dirt from her sleeve.

"Not exactly—but you can help us anyway. It's our uncle—"

"Oh, that dirty man!" cried Miss Sinknot. "I don't like to mention it, but his clothes were *not* clean and bright."

"Well," said Beth, "it's worse than that—he's missing!"

24

"Was he recaptured by the cobra?" gasped Miss Sinknot, removing some lint from her skirt.

"Who knows," sighed Beth, trying to look mournful. "But he's just plain disappeared."

"Oh my!" exclaimed Miss Sinknot. "How irresponsible! How might I be of assistance?"

"It's like this," explained Beth, "we want to file a missing person report on him, but the policeman inside won't listen to us because we're kids. But I bet if *you* gave him the information, he'd believe you."

"Yes," agreed Miss Sinknot. "Your uncle must be located swiftly so he may be properly sanitized! Lead me to the police officer and I shall do my duty."

"Great!" cheered Beth. "But it would be better if he didn't see us, so he won't know you're with us. We'll just wait in the hallway outside the office."

"But then how shall I provide the police officer with the proper information?" Miss Sinknot demanded.

"Um . . . I've got our uncle's business card here," replied Beth. "It's got his address and phone number and business number and all that kind of thing on it. And I'm sure you remember what he looked like."

"I certainly do—filthy from head to toe!" sniffed Miss Sinknot as we entered the police station.

"I don't get it," whispered Leo as we neared the Missing Persons Bureau. "How's this going to help?"

"Simple," Beth whispered back. "While Sinknot keeps the cop busy, we'll sneak behind him and see if the printout is still in the trash basket."

"I wish to file a missing person report on . . . John Smith," announced Miss Sinknot, consulting our uncle's business card.

"All right, all right," replied the policeman, starting to take down the information. As soon as we saw he was concentrating on listening and typing, we got to work. Leaving Teasdale in the hallway to keep guard, Leo sneaked around the left side of the room, and Beth took the right. We figured if one got caught, the other would still stand a chance.

While Miss Sinknot was describing our uncle in very unflattering terms, Beth got to the wastepaper basket. It was full almost to the brim, so it was hard to search for the printout quietly. At one point a stiff manila envelope rustled loudly, and the policeman looked around suspiciously.

But Beth was ready; before he could see her, she'd jumped backward and disappeared behind a file cabinet.

"Must've been mice," muttered the policeman.

"Mice!" gasped a horrified Miss Sinknot. "How unclean!"

Moments later Beth's search was rewarded; she was able to extract a large wad of paper from the basket. Across the top was printed:

### MISSING PERSON READOUT:
### AUGUST 6TH: CONFIDENTIAL!

Luckily for us, no one had emptied the trash since the day before. On tiptoe we left the room, without either Miss Sinknot or the policeman knowing we'd been there. Reconnoitering outside the door, we eavesdropped for a minute.

We heard a loud argument from inside the room:

"Listen, lady," the policeman was saying, "I just dialed the number on this business card you showed

26

me, and I got Mr. Smith himself. And he says he's not missing, never has been missing, and has no plans to ever be missing!''

"You must be misinformed," sniffed Miss Sinknot, spraying a spot on the desk as she spoke. "Doubtless the person to whom you spoke is an impostor, and the agent of the giant cobra who is holding the *real* John Smith hostage in the jungles of South America."

The policeman looked at Miss Sinknot as though she were a lunatic.

"Listen, lady," he said. "It's a federal crime to file an erroneous report."

"It's also a crime to have such a disgracefully dirty office!" cried Miss Sinknot, gesturing around her. "I would wager this place has not been properly sanitized in at least four months!"

The policeman shook his head and picked up the phone. "Get me the building guards," he said. "I've got a real loony bird here!"

"Well I never!" protested Miss Sinknot as we three kids fled giggling down the hall, the printout safe in Beth's grimy hand.

"What do you think'll happen to Miss Sinknot?" wondered Leo as we arrived at our uncle's apartment.

"They'll probably just think she made a mistake and let her go," reasoned Beth. "At least I hope so—she may be a pain, but I wouldn't want to get her in real trouble."

"Right," agreed Teasdale. "I don't think being in a prison cell would suit the neat Miss Sinknot well!"

"That's for sure!" laughed Beth. "Now let's see what this printout has to say."

# Chapter Five

# August 7th—Afternoon

"All right," began Beth. "Here goes. We can all look at it together." Spreading the printout on the table, we started to read:

*MISSING PERSON READOUT:*
*AUGUST 6TH: CONFIDENTIAL!*

*NAME: Sara Sanderson*
*DESCRIPTION: 5'8"; blonde; blue eyes; slim, age 35*
*LAST SEEN: New York City, three years ago*
*LAST KNOWN ADDRESS: 242 East 78th Street, New York, New York*
*ADDRESSES OF RELATIVES:*
  *1. Sidney Sanderson (Cousin)*
     *8 Gramercy Park South*
     *New York, New York*
  *2. Sassafras Sanderson (Aunt)*
     *19 Perry Street*
     *New York, New York*
  *3. Sartorius Sanderson (Uncle)*
     *196 West 89th Street*
     *New York, New York*

*FURTHER ADDRESSES:*
    *Reginald Varick (Family Lawyer)*
    *162 John Street*
    *New York, New York*
*FURTHER INFORMATION:*
    *The missing woman, Sara Sanderson, is believed to have disappeared of her own free will. It is not known if any of her relatives have heard from her; all deny any contact with Miss Sanderson. She is believed to have used aliases, but always retaining her initials, S.S. (Among her aliases have been Sondra Settle, Sally Sitwell, Shirley Snow.) It is not known what, if any, alias she is using now.*


*IMPORTANT NOTE:*
    *Vital to find Miss Sanderson on or before August 15th. This is imperative. This is the wish of Miss Sanderson's aunt, uncle, and cousin, each of whom has filed a missing person report on Miss Sanderson.*


"Christopher Columbus!" exclaimed Beth. "Who do you think this Sara Sanderson person is? Why did she vanish? And, boy—it's pretty bizarre how she matches up with that woman we made up. I'd say this is getting weirder by the minute."

"That's for sure," agreed Leo. "Why do you think everyone else who's looking for her wants her by August 15th, too? They couldn't all know it's our dad's birthday."

"Well," Beth sighed, "we were looking for a

mother, but I'd say we found a mystery instead. I say tomorrow we visit each of these addresses and find out what's up. The search for Sara Sanderson has just begun!''

MISS SINKNOT No. 2

# Chapter Six

# August 8th—
# Early Afternoon

Our first stop was 242 East 78th Street, Sara Sanderson's last known address. Locking up our bicycles against a parking meter, we paused a moment while Teasdale finished his banana.

Number 242 was an enormous brick residence, once elegant, now very run down. Vines wove their way 'round the fancy bow windows and paint was peeling from the wooden trim. Up on the third floor a few shutters were hanging at precarious angles, and we noticed some panes of glass had been broken.

It certainly didn't look like anyone was living in the house, but we rang the bell anyway.

"What do we say if someone answers?" demanded Leo.

"We'll think of something," replied Beth, ringing the bell again.

We heard the bell echoing from far away, deep inside the sleepy house, but no one came to answer the door.

We stood there and kept on ringing until it started to be embarrassing. An old lady in a light blue sweater passed by, looking at us curiously, and an odd man in a raincoat seemed to be staring at us from across the street.

We tried peering in the windows, but dark curtains had been drawn at each window, so there was nothing to see.

"There's no one here," announced Beth. "Let's try the next address."

Minutes later we were bicycling energetically down 78th Street, on our way to our next destination. Looking back over her shoulder, Beth could have sworn that the man with the raincoat was still staring at us.

Our next stop was a phone booth.

"Who lives here?" wondered Teasdale.

"Nobody, you silly!" laughed Beth. "I just wanted to see if the Sandersons' lawyer was in his office before we went all the way down to Wall Street. If he's anything like our dad, he's out a lot with clients."

"Christopher Columbus!" exclaimed Beth a minute later, hanging up the phone. "That's a mighty weird coincidence."

"What is?" Teasdale and Leo chimed in together.

"Listen to this: Reginald Varick, the Sandersons' lawyer, is out of town. But guess when he's coming back—August 15th! When I asked if they were sure he'd be back then, the secretary replied of course—on that day he has an important meeting he can't possibly miss."

"I wonder what's so special about August 15th," remarked Leo, scratching his elbow.

"Sooner or later," vowed Beth, "we're going to find out!"

*　　*　　*

After bicycling through Central Park, we found our way to 196 West 89th Street. It was an old brownstone, and looked even more run down than the house on East 78th Street. Among all the other beautifully maintained houses on the same block, it stuck out like a sore thumb.

A small handwritten sign next to the old-fashioned door knocker read: "Sartorius Sanderson, Esquire."

"Well, here we go," said Beth, knocking hard on the door.

"I'm coming, I'm coming!" cried a voice inside the house. "Don't knock the door down!"

Shuffling footsteps approached the door, an eye peered suspiciously through the peephole, and at last the door creaked open to reveal a bent old man. He had a large, shiny bald head, a small pointy goatee, and narrow bright eyes. He was wearing an incredibly ancient wrinkled suit, patched here and there with material that didn't match at all. He was so stooped over that although he was much taller than Beth, his head was exactly level with hers. Fixing her in his gaze, he shook his head angrily before speaking.

"If you're collecting money for some gimcrack cause, you can just skedaddle!"

"We're not collecting money," replied Beth. "We're—"

"Well then, I'll be a monkey's uncle if you're here to *give* me money!" interrupted the old gentleman. "Nor do I know you. And," he added, pausing for effect, "nor do I wish to! Good day." He started to close the door.

"Wait a minute!" cried Beth. "Are you Sartorius Sanderson?"

"What if I am?" queried the old man.

"Well, if you are," said Beth quickly, "then we're here on important family business."

"Family business, did you say?" said old Sartorius. "Then speak up or shut up!"

Beth spoke.

"It's about your niece, Sara Sanderson—" she began.

The old man looked suddenly very interested. "Sara," he muttered. "Well, I'll be! Step in, then," he continued, opening the door wide and ushering us inside.

Three mouths fell open when we saw the interior of Sartorius's house. What had surely once been a beautiful home now looked like a garbage dump. The rooms were filled up to the ceilings with junk, especially old newspapers. We had to weave our way through small alleys left between mountains of magazines that towered above us, all pitched at odd angles, all looking ready to collapse in a shower of dust.

We passed through three similarly cluttered rooms. In the fourth, the narrow passageway through the junk widened a bit and we saw three moldy fruit crates sitting on the floor.

"This is where I entertain guests," Sartorius told us, sitting down on the sturdiest crate.

Beth took the second crate and Teasdale and Leo shared the third.

"What is this business about Sara?" demanded Sartorius in a loud voice. "Does it involve money?"

Beth peered back at him and started feeling slightly

scared. Sartorius Sanderson looked insane, and the darkness of the room didn't help matters much. Although the day outside was bright with sunshine, almost no light found its way through Sartorius's dusty windows, and the little light that did was soon blocked by the piles of paper and trash. Only the faintest glimmer of light fell on Sartorius's eager, wrinkled face, causing deep shadows to form in his sunken cheeks and the hollows under his meager eyebrows.

Beth cleared her throat to give herself time to get her story straight in her own mind. Since we didn't know if we could trust any of the Sandersons, we'd decided not to tell them the truth. Beth had come up with a reason for us to be there, which wasn't the *best* reason in the world, but was the best she could think of at the time.

"It's like this," began Beth. "My brothers and I are volunteers at the public library—"

"Never go there," muttered Sartorius. "Too much to read right here at home!"

"So I see," said Beth, looking around her at the piles of old yellowed and crumbling newspapers. "Well—we're here because your niece, Sara Sanderson, has an overdue book which we're looking for."

"It's not here," Sartorius said sharply. Then, fiddling with his goatee, he looked Beth straight in the eye and demanded, "How did you know Sara Sanderson was my niece?"

"Um . . . um . . ." stalled Beth, thinking furiously. "Because she had to give references to get a library card, and she gave your name and wrote you were her uncle."

"I see," Sartorius remarked, still stroking his goatee and not looking entirely convinced. Furrowing his scanty eyebrows he suddenly demanded, "And exactly when was this book due?"

"Four years ago," explained Beth, an answer that seemed to relieve Sartorius.

"That makes sense," he said after a brief pause. "My niece has been missing for three years and in that time no one has seen hide nor hair of her."

"So you don't know where she is?" demanded Leo.

"I said she was missing, didn't I?" snapped Sartorius. "So of course I don't know where she is."

"One more thing," continued Beth, "if your niece doesn't return this book by a certain date, she'll have to pay a large fine."

"And when might this date be?" Sartorius asked.

"The fifteenth of August," Beth told him, watching Sartorius's expression as she said it.

For a fraction of a second the oddest expression flashed across Sartorius's face. It was impossible to tell whether it was fear, anger, or interest—but it was clear that the date August 15th meant something to him.

"I don't suppose that date means something to you," said Beth innocently.

"Not a thing!" vowed Sartorius. "And don't come running to me on that day, expecting me to pay my niece's fines for her! People who make their own beds should be prepared to lie in them."

"I see," said Beth. "One more thing—why did you file a missing person report on Sara?"

"Why shouldn't I?" demanded Sartorius. "It's a free country, isn't it?" He then muttered, "August 15," under his breath, an inscrutable look shadowing his face. "You'll have to leave," he said unexpectedly. "See yourselves out," he added. "Now go!"

We half-wanted to stay and explore but all of us were more anxious to get out of that strange house. Our dad always says we're the messiest people in the world, but he obviously never met Sartorius.

It took us ten minutes to navigate the maze of narrow tunnels and find the front door. Teasdale was getting claustrophobic, and when he gets claustrophobic he faints, so there was no time to lose.

When at last we reached sunlight, Teasdale gave an enormous sigh of relief and then pronounced:

"Although I don't know what he's done
I'm convinced Sartorius Sanderson
Has to be the villainous one!"

"He *is* pretty strange, but he's probably harmless enough," disagreed Leo, as Teasdale chewed on another banana.

While Beth and Leo unlocked our bicycles, Teasdale shared his banana with a chattering black squirrel. The squirrel, however, ate just a bite and threw the rest on the sidewalk.

"Don't bother to pick it up," Beth told Teasdale. "He'll probably come back for the rest once we're gone."

As we raced around the corner of 89th Street, turning south, Beth took a quick look behind her.

"Christopher Columbus!" she gasped. "Can it be?"
Stepping out from behind a lamp post, far up the
block, she saw a man in a raincoat, limping somewhat as he walked toward Sartorius's house . . .

# Chapter Seven

# August 8th—
# Late Afternoon

"Is Mr. Sanderson expecting you?" inquired the uniformed maid as we stood nervously in the elegant vestibule.

Behind us, out through the brightly polished oak door, the trees in Gramercy Park glittered in the August sunshine and the shouts of children playing made a nice contrast to the noise of the traffic beyond.

"Not exactly," admitted Beth. "But we're here on important business involving Mr. Sanderson's cousin, Sara."

The maid disappeared for two minutes, then returned. "Mr. Sanderson will see you now," she said.

Sidney Sanderson got up from his desk and met us by the door as the maid ushered us into his study.

He was in his early forties and quite handsome, well-dressed in an expensive suit. Smiling broadly, he asked us to sit down on some beautifully upholstered chairs. The whole room was stunningly—and expensively—furnished. From Teasdale's expression, Beth could tell he approved of Sidney Sanderson's taste in furniture. His taste in pictures was something else; on the wall behind him was a photograph of Sidney himself, posing next to a large stack of money, gazing at it with what looked like love in his eyes. And looking at him more closely, Beth noticed for the first time that his gold tie clip was in the shape of a dollar sign.

"It's a good thing for you you came today," explained Sidney. "Today just happens to be the one day a week I work at home . . . Now, what's all this about important business involving my cousin?"

"Hmmm," said Sidney when Beth had finished her speech about the overdue library book. "I'm afraid I'm unable to be of assistance." Pausing an instant, he continued, "I never knew the library sent out people to look so hard for lost or overdue books."

"Ah—you see it's cheaper than having to buy new ones," Beth told him. "We're volunteers, so we look for free."

"Most unusual," commented Sidney, looking at us carefully.

"So you're sure you don't know where your cousin is?" Leo asked.

"I only wish I did," Sidney replied.

"Why'd you file a missing person report on her?" demanded Beth. "And why'd you want her back by August 15th?"

"I filed a report because it was the only responsible thing to do," Sidney told us. "And I picked an arbitrary date—in this case, August 15th, because I thought the police might search more diligently if they thought they had a deadline to meet."

"So August 15th doesn't mean a thing to you otherwise?" Beth wanted to know.

"Not a thing," was the answer, delivered in a cool, steady voice. "Now," continued Sidney, "I have to return to work. I would, however, like to know your names—we somehow neglected to make proper introductions."

"Our names?" said Beth, who didn't want Sidney to know who we were.

"Yes—your and your brothers' names," repeated Sidney Sanderson in an even voice.

We answered all at once:

"Sylvia Soccerstar," said Beth.

"Pitter Wylie," said Teasdale.

"Cosmo Explorer," said Leo.

"Really?" Sidney remarked, arching an eyebrow. "How unusual for siblings to have different last names."

"Uh . . . we were adopted just yesterday," explained Beth desperately, "and we didn't have time to change our last names yet."

Sidney Sanderson gave an odd smile and rang for the maid to usher us out.

Leaving the building, Beth thought she saw the same stranger we'd seen earlier that day, lurking next to the fence enclosing Gramercy Park.

"Look sharp!" she told her brothers. "Doesn't he look familiar?"

But we weren't sure. The man we saw by the fence wasn't wearing a raincoat and had a large bandage on his forehead. No one remembered the man in the raincoat having a bandage.

"Who knows," said Beth. "But I do know two things: one, next time we get our fakes names coordi-

45

nated, and two, Sidney Sanderson is as guilty as they come! I bet a dollar he's up to something!''

''Why do you say that?'' Leo asked.

''Because anybody who loves money the way he seems to just has to be a villain!''

Perry Street turned out to be a quiet tree-lined street in Greenwich Village. We could see why this part of New York was called a village—the houses on the street were all neat little brownstones with nicely painted shutters and window boxes overflowing with flowers.

''I like it here,'' pronounced Beth as we searched for Number 19.

But just as old Sartorius's house didn't seem to fit on its block, so Number 19, the home of Sartorius's sister Sassafras, seemed out of place on hers. For one thing, while all the other houses seemed peaceful and quiet, there was a dreadful racket coming from Number 19. It sounded like millions of cats howling and millions of birds squawking. The house was also dilapidated; like Sartorius's, this house had clearly been neglected, and for a long time. Except for the din from inside, it looked even more abandoned than Sara's home had looked.

''Who's there?'' a quavering voice asked after Beth had given the door knocker, shaped like a cat's head, a few swift knocks on the peeling paint.

''We're here concerning your niece,'' replied Beth.

''My knees?'' wondered the voice on the other side of the door.

''Not your knees—your *niece,* Sara!'' Beth called.

''Something about Sara?'' said the voice, sounding

intrigued. The next thing we knew, a head popped out the open window near the door, just as a cat leaped up from the sidewalk and disappeared through the window.

Lively blue eyes examined us with interest and then the head vanished back through the window. Soon the door opened, and there stood a spry old woman. She had snow-white hair pulled back in a long ponytail, and high cheekbones accenting an ageless face devoid of makeup but full of mischief. She was wearing a floor-length gown of threadbare purple silk, and Beth noticed she was barefooted.

"I am Miss Sassafras Sanderson," she announced in a clear voice. "And to whom do I have the pleasure of speaking?"

"We're the Collins kids—Carlotta, Carl, and Casper," replied Beth, not especially liking lying to this friendly-looking woman. "We're volunteers from the New York Public Library."

"The library, you say?" repeated Sassafras. "My, how grand! An institution of great merit, that is what I believe the library to be. I go there whenever the opportunity presents itself. My guests adore being read to."

"Your guests?" asked Beth. "Who exactly are your guests?"

"Feline on the ground floor, ornithological on the third," explained Sassafras. "I myself live on the floor in between—to keep the peace, as it were."

"Huh?" wondered Beth. "I don't get it."

"Then by all means, come right in," chirped Sassafras with a smile. "All shall be made abundantly clear."

Passing through the entry hall, we entered the large living room which overlooked the street. In addition to a few sticks of furniture, it contained hundreds of cats: black ones, brown ones, Siamese, and tabbies. Countless kittens darted here and there, while more elderly cats dozed in faded overstuffed chairs. Lining one wall was a long row of saucers, some empty, some containing meat of some sort, the rest filled with milk or water.

Teasdale, who adores cats, had quickly noticed a skinny silver tabby and started petting it delightedly.

"Yes," smiled Sassafras, "this is my home for stray cats. I keep my windows open a cat-sized crack winter, summer, spring, and fall so no cat need ever sleep on the street who does not wish to. Food is provided too, of course, along with loving affection." And to prove the point, she picked up a fat tortoise-shell who'd been wrapping itself around her feet.

"And how are you today, Jawbone?" Sassafras asked the cat in her arms.

"Mrrrrouw," replied the cat.

"They all have names?" wondered Leo.

"Certainly they do!" replied Sassafras. "Imagine having a guest in one's home and not being able to call him or her by name. It would be most awkward. This one I call Jawbone because she always seems to be eating—so I imagined her jawbone must be frightfully strong."

Putting down Jawbone, Sassafras led us out of the room, shutting the door carefully behind us. We then proceeded up a grand, winding staircase, carpeted with a well-worn Indian rug. Up past the second floor we wound—"That's where I live," Sassafras told

**48**

us—and on up to the third. "This is where my other guests stay," said Sassafras.

Passing through a few doors, we at last entered a large room with windows looking down on the street in the front and a garden in the back. It seemed almost like a tree house, with branches waving outside all the windows. Actually, thought Beth, it seemed more like a tree—for there were as many birds in this room as there had been cats on the first floor. Robins, starlings, swallows, and others we didn't recognize fluttered round the long room, and nests had been built in lamps, on curtain rods, and onto moldings.

"This is my aerie," Sassafras said with a broad sweep of her arm. "I am quite sure being a bird in New York City is no easy task. Thus, I decided I would make a little hideaway for birds to come to when they wearied of the outdoor life. Of course, I get many more during the cold winter months, when the world outside is so unwelcoming."

As she spoke, a chickadee landed on her shoulder, while what looked to Teasdale like a chaffinch fluttered into a large pocket on her gown, produced a sunflower seed, and flew off merrily.

"Now," said Sassafras, "I do hope you'll join me for tea and tell me why you've called."

Tea was served in an old-fashioned parlor on the house's second floor. It was odd to sit and hear birdcalls—and to know they came not from outside, but from the floor above.

A maid appeared, dressed in a baggy old dress and a cap that hid all her hair and most of her face. She poured our tea and left.

"That is Olga," explained Sassafras, catching Beth staring at the maid. "She's Russian and has been with me for years. She does not care for strangers and is very shy around them. It can take her years to decide to speak to someone."

Following Beth's explanation of their visit, Sassafras shook her head sadly and said, "I am grieved to learn that my niece has been so negligent concerning her responsibility to the library. But, alas, she has disappeared, lo these many years, and alack, I myself simply do not have the money to pay whatever fine she may owe."

"Oh, don't worry about that," Beth put it quickly. "But tell me, have you any idea at all where your niece may be?"

"I?" said the old lady, looking suddenly nervous. "No, of course not—her whereabouts are a mystery to one and all."

"Why'd you file a missing person report on her?" demanded Leo.

"To locate her—I'm as anxious as anyone for my niece to be found," Sassafras replied.

"How about the date August 15th?" Beth persisted. "Does that mean anything to you?"

"I am quite sure it means nothing in the slightest," replied Sassafras, still looking nervous. "No," she added, "nothing whatsoever."

"Well, thank you, Miss Sanderson," said Beth as, later on, we were preparing to leave.

"Call me Sassafras," she said, giving each of us a light peck on the cheek.

\*     \*     \*

**51**

"It's her!" announced Leo as we headed home, walking our bikes as Teasdale said he was too tired to ride anymore in the August heat. "She's as crazy as a bedbug! I wouldn't be surprised if she'd spent time in a UFO and hadn't been the same since."

"Never," protested Teasdale. "I'd say she's kind and sweet, the dearest soul you could wish to meet."

"I liked her too," allowed Beth, as we neared our uncle's apartment on East 9th Street. "But I couldn't help but notice how everyone reacted when we mentioned August 15th—except for Sidney, and he's so cool a customer he wouldn't get excited in an earthquake!"

"Yes," agreed Leo. "One or all of those three is hiding something—I just wish we knew who, and what it is they're hiding."

"That's precisely what we're going to find out," vowed Beth. "And we'll find Sara Sanderson, too— and by August 15th!"

MISS SINKNOT No. 3

52

## Chapter Eight

# August 8th—Evening (from the diary of Fudge Ferrara)

What a day! If I never see those three kids again, it'll be too soon. I think something's wrong with them. And I think they're out to get me. I'm black and blue! The Boss said to trail them, so I did. Somehow they must have wised up to the fact. I wonder how. I was all disguised in a raincoat like a real spy.

I started trailing them yesterday, outside the police station. I guess they were ready for me. Some weird dame who seems to know them threw a banana peel on the ground and later, when I was running to see where they went, I slipped on it. I fell real hard and hurt my leg. It made me limp so I couldn't catch up with the little creeps. But Joe in the station said they didn't come up, just the weird dame. He said she was a real nut case. And before the station guards could heave her out, she ran from the station screaming about something being clean and bright.

Anyway, I followed those weird kids all day today. Uptown I saw 'em on the Upper West Side and would have been able to get real close to 'em. But I fell into the trap they left for me—I slipped on a piece of banana and fell real hard on my head. So I had to go home and bandage it up. But then when I left to go out again I forgot my raincoat so I guess my disguise was ruined. I caught up with 'em later—the little crooks.

Anyway, the Boss says things don't look good, with those dumb kids poking around. Yeah—my Boss's worst fears have come true—those kids saw not only my Boss, but the other Sandersons too! We want to know who they're working for. We want to know everything they know. Maybe they could lead us to *her*—somebody has to know where Sara Sanderson is! Maybe they do. My Boss says to follow the kids til' we know what they're up to. I can't wait to get my hands on those little good-for-nothings! But now I gotta soak my sore leg and change the bandage on my forehead.

Those kids! I always said no kids can outdo me. I'm gonna get a good night's sleep so I'll be ready for 'em the next time I see 'em.

# Chapter Nine

# August 9th—Evening

A sliver of moon lit the sky over Manhattan. Further down the street a dark form lurched homeward while a large truck rattled along the avenue up ahead.

It was two in the morning and East 78th Street was just about deserted.

"Christopher Columbus!" whispered Beth. "I never knew New York could be so quiet."

"I say it's *too* quiet," replied Leo, shivering a bit.

Teasdale was saying nothing at all—he was too nervous to speak.

Soon we were standing in front of the deserted brownstone where Sara Sanderson used to live. "Maybe we could find some clues in Sara's old house," Beth had suggested earlier that day, so we decided to return to the house at night, to break in and see what we could find. We'd waited until we were sure our uncle was fast asleep. He'd have grounded us for life if he'd caught us going out in the middle of the night.

After trying the door—locked, of course—we approached the windows, each taking one. Perching ourselves on the broad window ledges, each of us tried our window. Beth and Leo tugged at theirs, trying to force the bottom half of the frame upward—but although the old wood creaked with the strain, the windows remained shut tight.

"Mine seems shut with glue," Teasdale called to us in a low voice, "There's nothing I can do." He turned to go, lost his balance, and went tumbling back against the window. Leo and I watched in horror as the whole window frame gave way with a splintering groan. Then, with a small shriek accompanied by the sound of breaking glass and a dull thud, Teasdale disappeared into the black empty house.

"Teas!" cried Beth. "We're coming!"

Leaping through the gaping hole where the window had been, we found Teasdale lying spread-eagle on top of the window frame, which itself was lying on the floor. Splinters of wood and shards of glass were everywhere Beth shone her flashlight.

"Am I alive?" asked Teasdale in a quavering voice.

We assured him he was, and helped him to his feet and checked him out for injuries. Then we set to exploring the quiet house—but the quiet was soon broken by a heartrending cry from Teasdale.

"Ghosts!" he gasped, looking around him and promptly collapsing against a wall.

"Where?" asked Leo, peering about anxiously.

"Nowhere!" chuckled Beth, taking a moment to reassure her brothers. We'd ended up in what was apparently the living room, and all the pieces of furniture had been draped in white sheets to keep off dust. The sheets *did* make the furniture look a bit like ghosts.

"It looks as though they've kept all of Sara's old

stuff," surmised Beth. "Perhaps that means they're expecting her back sometime."

Leaving the living room, we tiptoed down a long narrow hallway. The wooden floor creaked as we found our way along it, while the small beam of light cast by Beth's flashlight barely seemed to make a dent in the darkness.

At the far end of the hallway stood a door.

"Don't open it!" begged Teasdale. "Who knows what's behind it!" Teasdale does tend to worry, so Beth tried to calm him.

"Oh, Teasdale, don't fret—there's no one here but us!"

With a shove from Beth and Leo, the door opened, its hinges squeaking loudly, and we saw we were standing at the entrance to the dining room. From the doorway, Beth aimed her flashlight slowly around all four corners of the room.

"See, Teasdale," she said. "All that's in this room is this old table, and these chairs, covered in sheets like everything else in this place."

"Maybe there's a monster hiding under the table!" suggested Teasdale in a faint voice.

"No way!" replied Beth—and bravely strode over to the table, lifted the sheet, and shone her light in.

"See?" she called. "There's no one here but us kids!"

As we slowly made our way around the dining room, heading toward a door on the far side, Leo suddenly called out, "Freeze, everybody!"

We froze.

Leo, now caught in the light of Beth's flashlight, seemed to be listening with all his strength, just as though the dark house were hiding some secret he could almost, but not quite, hear.

"Leo, what is it?" demanded Beth.

Pausing, and looking around before replying, Leo finally said, "I thought I heard something."

"What kind of something?" wondered Teasdale, too nervous to rhyme.

"It sounded like something moving around," whispered Leo.

"It was probably just your imagination," replied Beth. "You know how old houses make funny noises."

The kitchen stood on the other side of the dining-room door. Its one piece of furniture, a round table, was draped with a piece of old material in place of a sheet.

The old house suddenly seemed extra silent. In fact, the whole world seemed to be holding its breath: The plane trees outside the kitchen window stopped rustling their leaves and a siren's mournful wail faded away into nothingness.

Then Teasdale interrupted the silence.

"Beth, Leo," he said in a low voice. "There's something under that table!"

"Oh, Teasdale!" reprimanded Beth. "Save your imagination for your poetry."

And with a dramatic gesture, Beth yanked the cloth off the table and shone her light underneath.

"Aaaaaaah!" screamed Beth. "There's something there!" Soon Teasdale and Leo were screaming too. The next second, Beth, in her fright, dropped the flashlight, plunging the kitchen into complete darkness.

We were now running around in circles, looking

for the exit, but succeeding only in knocking into one another.

Suddenly whoever it was who'd been under the table grabbed the fallen flashlight, switched it back on, and was shining it into our eyes.

Hugging each other in fear, the three of us were virtually blinded by the light. We couldn't see who it was we were up against.

"Don't hurt us!" beseeched Beth. "We're only kids!"

"And what might you be doin' here?" asked a woman's voice. She sounded both scared and angry, and the voice appeared to have an accent.

"We were taking a walk and took a wrong turn," cried Beth desperately.

"Aye, and pigs can fly!" mocked the voice. "You'd best be tellin' me what you're doin' here before I go an' call the police."

Beth decided it was time for the truth.

"We're searching for Sara Sanderson," she explained.

"And why might you be doin' that?" asked the voice.

"We're not really sure," Beth had to admit.

"Not really sure, are you?" the voice repeated. "Tell me more."

"The saints preserve us!" cried the voice when Beth had finished her explanation. "So you're not burglars after all—only children tryin' to do good."

She walked over to the wall and switched on the overhead light. We saw the owner of the voice was an elderly woman with bright pink cheeks, a round face, and gray hair pulled into a bun. We recognized her as

the woman in the blue sweater we'd noticed on the street the day before.

"I am Bridget O'Sheehan," she said. "I was Sara's nanny when she was a wee slip of a thing. Then later, when she was all upped and grown, I became her maid. Not that she ever let me do much work, mind you. Aye, I've been with the Sandersons for thirty-three years, ever since I came over from Ireland."

"But where's Sara now?" Beth demanded. "What's happened to her?"

"If only I knew," sighed Bridget. "My heart's broken, it is, since she disappeared without a word."

"Do you think she's all right?" Leo wanted to know.

"Oh, I know she's all right," Bridget replied. "For twice a year, just like clockwork, she sends me a card, tellin' me so. On my birthday and on Christmas—she never forgets. But the postmarks are always different, so I have no way of knowin' if she's movin' around all the time, or has friends in faraway places mail them for her."

"But why did she go?" asked Beth.

"Well," began Bridget, "I'd say it all began when Sara's parents died in that terrible accident. She was only twelve at the time and of course she took it hard. She and I continued livin' in this house, but officially, Sara was the ward of her Uncle Sigmund."

"Sigmund?" interrupted Beth. "We haven't met him."

"I should hope not," continued Bridget, "seeing as how he died three years ago!"

"Three years ago!" interrupted Beth again. "Christopher Columbus! That's when Sara disappeared!"

**61**

"That's right. And I didn't understand it until only two weeks ago," volunteered Bridget. "I've been simply burstin' to tell someone, but I didn't know who I could trust! I knew one of the Sandersons had a friend on the police force, someone named Joe, I believe—so I didn't want to go there. I didn't know which of the Sandersons I could rely on. They're a mighty odd lot—daft, the whole bunch of them! Old Mr. Sartorius is mad over his old junk, old Miss Sassafras can't live without her birds and cats, and young Mr. Sidney lives for money! I didn't know where to turn!"

"You can trust us," cried Beth.

"I believe I can," Bridget said. "Well—two weeks ago I was at Mr. Varick's office. He's the Sandersons' lawyer, you know. Ever since Miss Sara disappeared, I go to him twice a month to draw my salary for taking care of this house. He refuses to send it to me; he makes me take the trip to see him. And just for spite, I'd say—he's not a nice man. Well, there I was, sittin' in his office, waitin' to be paid, and I happened to overhear him talkin' with his secretary. I wasn't eavesdroppin', mind you—no, they'd left the intercom on. And I think I know why young Miss Sara left so sudden."

"Why?" we gasped.

"The will," said Bridget simply. "Old Sigmund's will—he left everything to Sara. All thirty million."

"But what's wrong with that?" asked Beth.

"Ah—but it isn't that simple," Bridget told us. "Old Mr. Sigmund was as strange a duck as his brother Sartorius and his sister Sassafras. And he left a strange will, which said that the only way Sara could inherit all his millions would be to show up at his lawyer's office three years after his death, on August 15th."

"Why August 15th?" wondered Leo.

"It happened to be his parents' weddin' anniversary, and he was devoted to them."

"I still don't get why that would make Sara want to disappear," Beth asked Bridget.

"Ah—if you just hold on, you'll see. I also learned that if Sara didn't show up, then the thirty million would be divided equally among the remainin' relatives—in this case, Sartorius, Sassafras, and Sidney."

"There are no other relatives?" demanded Beth.

"None," replied Bridget.

"But I still don't see why that would make Sara want to run away," persisted Beth.

"Let me explain, child," said Bridget patiently. "You see, my theory is that Sara knew it would be worth the while of her relatives to get rid of her—it'd be worth ten million dollars to each of them. Well do I remember her sayin' to me, 'Bridget—there's one relative of mine I just don't trust! One who'd stop at nothin' to get more money—even murder!' So I'm thinkin' she decided to lay low until the three years were up."

"So then everything will turn out all right!" cheered Beth.

"I hope so," Bridget sighed. "But with such peculiar folks involved—I don't trust that lawyer Varick any more than I trust the Sandersons—who knows if Sara was even given the right date to show up at Varick's office? And if she doesn't show up, she'll be

63

cheated out of her rightful inheritance, and there's nothin' I can do about it!''

Poor Bridget began to weep. We put our arms around her and told her not to worry—we'd find Sara, if anyone could. And if we couldn't, we'd think of something else.

"There's still something I don't understand," said Beth when Bridget had calmed down somewhat. "Why do you think Sartorius, Sassafras, and Sidney filed missing person reports on Sara, all saying she had to be found by August 15th?"

Bridget considered a moment before replying.

"I'm afraid one of them—the one Sara didn't trust—might want to find her before the fifteenth—to stop her from showin' up! She could be in real danger!" After wiping a few tears from her eyes, Bridget continued, "Of course, there's also the chance that one or two of the Sandersons is trying to *help* Sara. I only wish I knew who was up to what."

"I bet old Sartorius is behind the crime," announced Teasdale. "A poor guy like him needs money all the time."

"Poor?" gasped Bridget. "Mr. Sartorius is as rich as a king—he's just crazy. He needs more money like he needs more newspapers."

"I say it's Sidney—he certainly loves money," reasoned Beth.

"That's true," admitted Bridget. "But as far as I know, he's a very successful businessman. Why should he commit a crime to get more money? He'd be riskin' everythin' he already has—it doesn't make sense."

"That's for sure," agreed Leo. "That's why I say it's Sassafras. I bet she's broke."

"I don't know for sure," said Bridget. "But I do know she inherited a good deal of money some years ago. I imagine she must have some money left—how else could she pay for all that cat food and birdseed?"

"Well, it has to be one of them," commented Beth. "And we'll find out which—and we'll find Sara, too!"

"Oh, I hope you can!" cried Bridget. "My only two wishes in life are to see Miss Sara again and to set foot one more time on the good Irish soil of County Cork!"

We were just saying good-bye to Bridget when the old Irishwoman burst out, "I've got an idea about how we might find Miss Sara!"

"How?" we asked.

"I was readin' the newspaper this afternoon, and I noticed it was filled with ads of people lookin' for people. And I remembered that Miss Sara used to read them—not that she was a-lookin' to meet people, but just because she found them interestin'. So I'm thinkin' you could maybe put an ad in lookin' for Sara—but carefully worded, mind you, so only she would understand it. I'd thought of doin' it a year or two ago, but Miss Sara had written me not to go lookin' for her. She wrote it would only lead to trouble. But now, with August 15th less than a week away, I'd say we'd have nothin' to lose by tryin'. Will you do it?"

"First thing in the morning," replied Beth.

"Oh, bless you dear children!" cried Bridget, giving each of us a warm embrace. "And be careful—those Sandersons are an odd bunch!"

It was past three A.M. when we left the house. Halfway down the block, Beth suddenly motioned for her brothers to be still.

"I see something!" she whispered. "Between those two parked cars! I'm sure I saw someone jump down quickly."

"Let's go in the other direction," said Teasdale nervously, slowly edging away from where Beth was pointing.

We turned to follow Teasdale when without warning he gave a bloodcurdling yelp and disappeared behind a parked mini-van.

"Teasdale!" we shrieked. "Where are you?"

The only response was a muffled cry for help, so in a flash we raced over to the van, our hearts beating madly and our fists ready for battle.

But in place of a mugger we saw Miss Sinknot. She had Teasdale firmly in her strong grasp and was furiously wiping his face with a rag.

"Clean and bright, clean and bright," she was chanting, "in the daytime and in the night!"

"Go clean someone your own size!" we cried angrily, leaping on Miss Sinknot and freeing a shaken Teasdale.

"But I had not yet finished cleaning him properly!" cried Miss Sinknot in a fury. She began madly spraying in our direction with her can of Lysol—but by that time we were far down the street, running as fast as our legs could carry us!

# Chapter Ten

# August 10th—Evening (from the diary of Fudge Ferrara)

It's almost midnight, and the Boss is hopping mad. Here's what happened so far: I followed those kids to the old Sanderson place and saw one of them fall into a window. What a clod! I decided to wait outside for them. I was hiding between two parked cars when all of a sudden that same weird dame I saw them with outside the police station appears from behind a mini-van and starts spraying everything with something in a can. You better bet I got outta there quick! I'm no fool. Who knows what that woman's got in that can?

Anyway, the Boss called in a fit about what's in tonight's paper. I cut out the ad and here it is:

Attention all blonde women! Are you five foot eight and fond of the letter "S"? Do you have blue eyes? Does August 15th mean something special to you? Are you around thirty-five? If so, please call 555-8848 and ask for Lethdale. Thank you.

The Boss wants to know what those little stinkers are up to now. And is that old maid in on it too? The

67

Boss says we gotta take care of that old servant. And then we gotta find out everything those kids know, and take care of them too. I can't wait to see the last of them! I'm still limping and my head's still sore. I knew I didn't like kids. Now I gotta make a phone call: The Boss says I gotta have two strong guys to help me get those kids. I think I'll call Fuzzy and Footsy. And the Boss says there's a job for a woman, too. I'll have to call Fannie.

That's all for now.

# Chapter Eleven

# August 11th—Morning & Afternoon

Our dad phoned while we were eating breakfast.

"Are you being good?" he wanted to know.

"We've never been better," replied Beth.

"Glad to hear it," said our dad. "Well, I'll be picking you up at Uncle John's on the evening of the fifteenth. Will you kids have enough to keep you busy until then?"

"I guess so," answered Beth.

"Good!" said our dad. "And remember—keep out of trouble!"

"That's exactly what we're trying to do," Beth told our dad—and moments later was joining Teasdale and Leo as we headed out the door, bound for further investigations.

We'd decided to return to Sara Sanderson's house to talk with Bridget again. "I'd like to know which of the Sandersons she suspects," Beth had said. "I'd say no one knows that family better than Bridget."

"Maybe so," Leo had answered, "but I still say Sassafras is behind all this."

"I say it's Sidney," disagreed Beth.

"And I say Sartorius," Teasdale told us. "And I know I'm right, so don't make a fuss."

But though we pounded on the door and hollered like crazy, no one answered. We began to get worried that something might have happened to Bridget, so we decided to let ourselves in. Luckily, while the window Teasdale had fallen through had been repaired somewhat, it still was shaky, so forcing our way in wasn't difficult.

"It's a good thing we're not burglars," commented Beth as we entered the house.

We found our way to the kitchen, but there was still no sign of Bridget.

"Christopher Columbus!" exclaimed Beth, reading a note she'd found on the kitchen table. "I guess we can't ask Bridget anything."

"Why not?" asked Leo.

"Just take a look," replied Beth, handing the note to her brothers.

Teasdale and Leo gathered closer and read the following:

Dear Children,

I'm sorry not to be here to see you again. But in case you came back, I decided to leave you a note. Well—the most wonderful thing has happened! It's so grand I can barely believe it. I've been given a free round trip ticket to Ireland! I leave the morning of the eleventh and don't know yet when I'll return. It's the dream of my life! The ticket came in the mail. It didn't say who it was from—but I'd say it had to have been Miss Sara. What do you think?

I'll send you a postcard. You three be careful! And remember—those Sandersons are an odd bunch. I do hate to leave—I'm just so sure Sara's life is in danger. Please keep trying to find her. God be with you.

Your friend,
Bridget O'Sheehan

P.S. Beware of S.S.!

"A fat lot of help this is," grumbled Leo. "All the Sandersons have 'S.S.' for their initials."

"That's for sure," agreed Beth. "We're still back where we started."

"Well," considered Leo, "at least old Bridget got her trip to Ireland. That sure was nice of Sara."

"If it *was* Sara," snorted Beth.

"What do you mean?"

"I mean it's all a little too convenient," Beth explained. "I say someone just wanted to get Bridget out of the way before she told us too much."

"Yes," agreed Teasdale, "there can be little doubt—someone wanted Bridget out."

"Well, boys," asked Beth that afternoon, "what have you discovered?"

We'd split up after leaving Sara's old house: Teasdale stood watch by Sartorius's house, Leo by Sassafras's, and Beth by Sidney's.

"Nothing much happened at Sassafras's," reported Leo. "She received a large shipment of birdseed and was so happy she gave the truck driver a twenty-dollar tip."

71

"That proves she's not broke," said Beth.

"Or," countered Leo, "it could mean that she knows she's going to get all that money in four days and she's spending what she has without worrying about it."

"Hmmm," Beth considered. "Maybe. Anyway—I hid by Sidney's study window and did some eavesdropping. I heard Sidney speaking on the phone—and he seemed very excited about some money he was about to make. Now, I'd say *that* was suspicious."

Leo disagreed. "No," he said, "if Sidney's a successful businessman, the way Bridget said he was, why shouldn't he make money? What you heard doesn't prove anything."

"I guess not," admitted Beth. "How about you, Teasdale?"

"I stood watch by Sartorius's house,
And I can say he is a louse!
Some papers were delivered—not a few, but many!
And he didn't tip the deliverer a penny!"

"What a cheapskate!" observed Beth. "But it still doesn't prove he's a crook. I guess we haven't discovered too much today."

"Well, at least Miss Sinknot didn't show up to sanitize us," said Leo.

"Right," agreed Beth, "and that strange guy in the raincoat must have taken the day off."

But none of us really felt cheerful—there were only three days left until August 15th, and we were getting nowhere fast!

# Chapter Twelve

# August 12th—Morning

We were so anxious to be on time that we arrived at Times Square half an hour early.

"Let's have a lemonade and think things over," suggested Beth.

We certainly had enough to think over—it had been an eventful morning. It all began at nine—just after our uncle had left for the day—when Beth went to answer the phone.

"I'm calling about your ad in the newspaper," said a woman's voice.

"Great!" Beth replied. "Are you—"

"Ssshh!" the voice interrupted. "I can't talk now! And especially not over the phone!"

"But—"

"Listen," continued the voice, "I'm going to give you an address and I want you to meet me there at eleven-thirty. The address is 235 West 43rd Street, right near Times Square. It's an office building. I'll be waiting for you in Suite 2-31—it's on the second floor. Don't be late—and don't tell anyone you're coming!"

"Who are—" began Beth, but the party on the other end had hung up.

"What did she sound like?" asked Leo as we made our way to a luncheonette we'd spotted near the corner of 44th Street.

"Who?" Beth wondered.

"Sara Sanderson, of course," Leo replied. "Who else would answer the ad?"

"That," said Beth, "is what we are soon going to find out!"

"I'm sorry, but we're out of lemonade," said the skinny waitress.

"Then we'll have orange juice," Beth replied.

"We're out of that, too," said the waitress.

"How about grapefruit juice?" wondered Leo.

"All gone," sighed the waitress.

"What's going on around here?" demanded Beth. "How can you be out of juice so early in the day?"

"Because of *her!*" replied the waitress. "It's that blimp in the corner—she's only been in here twenty minutes, but so far she's consumed about ten gallons of fruit juice and lemonade, not to mention an entire truckload of bagels."

Following the direction of the waitress's gaze, we looked over to the far corner of the luncheonette—and there we saw an enormous woman in a little red beret, sitting alone at a table and surrounded by at least seventy empty glasses and a small stack of empty plates.

"Christopher Columbus!" gasped Beth. "It's Mrs. Fillipelli!"

"You're right!" agreed Leo, and the three of us

dashed over to say hello to our old friend. We'd met Mrs. Fillipelli in New Hampshire when we'd gone on a little holiday with our Aunt Henrietta, and Mrs. Fillipelli had helped us solve a mystery. She was the fattest person we'd ever known, as well as the jolliest.

"Well, land sakes alive!" bellowed Mrs. Fillipelli when she'd caught sight of us. "If it isn't my old buddies, the Three Musketeers!"

Sitting down at Mrs. Fillipelli's table, we were soon all up to date with our old friend.

"So you're solving mysteries again?" boomed Mrs. Fillipelli. "There's just no stopping you kids, is there?" She then gave an immense laugh and slapped her hefty thigh with enthusiasm.

It turned out Mrs. Fillipelli was also early for an appointment, and in the same building where we were supposed to meet "Sara Sanderson."

After Mrs. Fillipelli had paid her bill—which was gigantic—the four of us walked over to West 43rd Street together.

"My appointment's at eleven-fifteen," confided Mrs. Fillipelli, "and it shouldn't take more than fifteen minutes or so—I'm just putting in an order with an Italian importing company. They import the tastiest little cookies!"

"How much are you buying?" asked Leo.

Mrs. Fillipelli gave a broad grin, patted her sizable stomach, and replied, "Oh—only half a ton!"

Mrs. Fillipelli invited us out for lunch in her favorite Italian restaurant, and we made plans to meet after our appointments.

"I bet you'll be done before we are," considered Beth. "Why don't you wait for us in the lobby?"

75

"Too dull!" said Mrs. Fillipelli, shaking her head so vigorously that her mountain of chins shook like real mountains during a major earthquake.

"Where then?" we asked.

"How about the elevator?" suggested Mrs. Fillipelli. "I simply adore elevators—I could ride in 'em forever! Up and down, up and down—where else can I go up and down so easily?"

"Sounds good to me," smiled Leo.

"Oh—one more thing," announced Mrs. Fillipelli, "just in case *you* have to wait for *me*." She delved in her large pocketbook and produced a plastic bag full of chocolate chip cookies. "Made 'em myself!" she boasted. "And are they a taste sensation!" She gave each of us three cookies, which we put in our pockets.

"Thanks," said Beth. "We'll see you soon—in the elevator."

At exactly eleven-thirty we entered the building and found our way to Suite 2-31. Beth knocked loudly on the door.

"Who's there?" called a woman's voice.

"Us!" cried Beth. "The kids who put the ad in the paper."

The door opened swiftly and a woman ushered us into an office, empty except for a desk with some sandwiches on it. The woman who'd let us in looked around fifty and had short reddish hair and bloodshot green eyes. She was also nowhere near five foot eight—she was probably closer to five foot two.

"You can't be Sara Sanderson!" said Beth in a stunned voice.

"Who said I was, girlie?" replied the woman, locking the door behind us in one swift motion.

"Then why'd you answer our ad?" demanded Beth.

"Shut up!" snapped the woman, calling over her shoulder, "C'mon, Fudge—they're here!"

Before we could figure out what was happening, a door on the far wall of the room burst open and three men came through it. In their hurry to get in, one tripped over another's feet and fell with a thud to the floor. We recognized him as the man in the raincoat who'd been following us around!

We made a mad dash for freedom—but too late! A man with ugly fuzzy hair leaped on Teasdale, another with feet the size of Pennsylvania tripped Leo and pinned him to the floor, while the third, the one we'd recognized, managed to get hold of Beth.

We fought like wildcats, especially Beth. Even Teasdale threw some mighty punches and yanked at his captor's fuzzy hair while Beth kicked and punched the one who'd grabbed her. Leo was too pinned down to fight.

But they were just too strong for us, and before long they'd tied our hands behind our backs and bound our ankles together.

"No one's gonna hurt you—for now!" said the man we'd seen before. He seemed to be the leader, which was hard to believe because he also seemed incredibly stupid.

"That's tellin' 'em, Fudge!" said the one with the fuzzy hair.

"Thanks, Fuzzy," said Fudge. "Now, uh . . . what do we do next?"

"I thought *you* knew," said Fuzzy, scratching his

scalp. "What do you think, Footsy?" he asked the guy with enormous feet.

Footsy, who was busy practicing tying his shoe-laces, didn't appear to hear the question.

"Footsy!" hollered Fuzzy. "Answer me when I ask you a question!"

"That's it!" Fudge shouted with delight. "We're supposed to ask the little creeps questions!" Reaching into his pocket he produced a piece of paper. "In fact," continued Fudge, "the Boss even gave me a list!"

"Who's your Boss?" demanded Beth.

"Can it!" replied Fudge. "I get to ask the questions—not you!"

Consulting his list, with eyes narrowed and forehead furrowed as he attempted to read, Fudge finally said:

"List of questions."

"Uh, Fudgy," said the woman, whose name turned out to be Fannie, and whose voice Beth recognized as the one on the telephone that morning, "I don't think you're supposed to read that part—that's just the heading!"

"Oh," Fudge replied. "I get it. Here we go: Question one—why are you looking for Sara Sanderson?"

"None of your business," answered Beth.

"I guess I better write down their answers," said Fudge. Grabbing a pencil he started writing "None of your business."

A quick conference among Fudge, Fuzzy, Footsy, and Fannie ensued. When it was done, Fudge said:

"That answer's no good! Tell me why you're looking for Sara Sanderson!"

"Never in a million years!" vowed Leo.

Fannie quickly whispered to Fudge that that answer was no good either, so Fudge repeated the question. This time, Teasdale answered:

> "I won't answer your question, sir,
> Till cats can fly and fish have fur!"

"Huh?" said Fudge.

Another conference took place. When it was over, Fannie left, saying, "I'm just too softhearted to watch what happens next!"

"She looks as softhearted as a piranha," whispered Beth.

"Hey, Fannie," Fudge called out, "remember to distract the operator for, oh, five minutes."

While we were still trying to figure this remark out, Fudge turned to us and said, "All right—I'll give you one last chance to answer my questions."

"Forget it!" announced Beth.

"Then we're gonna scare the answers out of you," Fudge replied.

"We don't scare easily," boasted Beth.

"We'll see about that!" menaced Fudge. And, nodding to Fuzzy and Footsy, he and his cohorts proceeded to gag us and drag us out of the office into the hallway.

Footsy pressed the elevator call button. When it arrived he got in and managed to lower the elevator a few feet. Fuzzy and Fudge meanwhile kept the door open, revealing the top of the elevator. They pulled Footsy out and soon put us in—on *top* of the elevator! We were bound together so securely we couldn't

budge, and gagged so tightly we couldn't make a sound.

Fudge grinned at us and said, "We're just gonna let you ride up and down for a while—that oughta scare you good! Maybe after an hour you'll answer our questions!"

Then he let the doors slide shut—plunging us into near darkness. There we were, the three of us, bound and gagged, riding on top of an elevator in the eerie blackness of an elevator shaft! And no one but Fudge and his friends knew we were there!

First the elevator went down.

Riding on top of an elevator feels very different from riding inside one. To begin with, you're riding in near darkness, and second, the noises all around you are strange and frightening—long pulleys groan and whine, odd cords crack as they extend and tighten, and the wind trapped in the long tall shaft moans and whistles like a mechanical ghost.

Then the elevator started going up.

Initially, this seemed better than going down: The elevator, an old one, moved relatively slowly, so we didn't have that queasy feeling in the pit of our stomachs we got when it was going down. Also, since we'd been placed on the elevator flat on our backs, we could see where we were going.

The building we were in was nineteen stories tall, so at first we couldn't see the top of the elevator shaft—the shaft was too dark, and the top too far away.

But as the elevator gradually rose, the top started

becoming visible, a dim square of white concrete looming far above us.

Beth then became aware that Leo was squirming like mad and trying to say something. Beth could tell by the wild look in Leo's eyes that it was very important. But what was it?

Looking over at Teasdale, Beth was relieved to discover he'd fainted. "At least *he's* out of it," she thought to herself.

Slowly the elevator rose. Dimly, from inside the elevator, we could hear the voice of the operator. "So that's who Fannie was distracting," thought Beth.

"Tenth floor," the operator called out, and, a few moments later, "Twelfth floor."

We tried calling out for help—but with the gags on we couldn't be heard over the grinding of machinery. We also tried pounding on the top of the elevator, but tied as tightly as we were, we couldn't produce much noise.

"Sixteenth floor," called the operator, and Leo looked more and more panicked.

"Seventeenth floor," called the operator—and suddenly, horribly, Beth realized why Leo was so frightened.

"This can't be!" she thought as the elevator rose slowly, jerking its way toward the building's nineteenth floor.

But it was.

Fudge had been too dumb to figure out that if the elevator was called to the nineteenth floor, we would be crushed against the square of concrete Beth had noticed above us earlier.

"Eighteenth floor," Beth heard the operator announce. "Next stop, the nineteenth floor!"

Up rose the elevator—up toward the nineteenth floor. Closer and closer loomed the top of the building; higher and higher rose the elevator; nearer and nearer grew the concrete slab. It seemed to be waiting there just to crush the life out of us!

Slowly but surely the elevator continued upward—with us on top, headed for certain death!

# Chapter Thirteen

# August 12th—
# Afternoon

The concrete roof was now just inches away, and the whirring mechanism of the elevator was bringing us closer and closer. Soon our noses were almost brushing the concrete.

Then, with the concrete roof flush against our heads, the mechanism lifting the elevator gave a horrendous groan, and the elevator quivered slightly and came to a dead halt.

Now that the elevator shaft was silent, we could make out the conversation inside the elevator.

"What's going on?" cried a nervous passenger.

"Are we trapped?" wondered another.

"Please remain calm," said the operator firmly. "I think I know what's wrong—the elevator is over-loaded. We'll have to go back down to the eighteenth floor and let someone out—"

"But I want to go to the nineteenth floor!" interrupted a passenger irritably. "And I don't want to walk up! I'm carrying a heavy package!"

"No one'll have to walk," sighed the operator.

"We'll just let some people off on eighteen and come back for them later."

"You should let off the fat one," instructed a passenger rudely.

"Yeah," cried another. "She must weigh five hundred pounds! I'm amazed the elevator moves at all with *her* in it!"

"Uh, ma'am," we heard the operator say, and we knew he had to be speaking to Mrs. Fillipelli, "you'll have to get off on the eighteenth floor. You've been riding up and down in this elevator for over fifteen minutes anyway. Where do you want to go?"

"I happen to be meeting friends," explained Mrs. Fillipelli.

"In an elevator?" a passenger wanted to know.

"Obviously," answered Mrs. Fillipelli.

Next we heard the pulleys come to life, and over their dull roar the operator announced, "We're going down to eighteen!" And sure enough, the elevator slowly descended, and our heads were no longer scraping the concrete above us. For the moment we were saved.

In an instant we'd reached the floor below.

"Okay, ma'am," said the operator, "you'll have to get out so I can take these passengers to the nineteenth floor."

"I will not!" Mrs. Fillipelli replied in a loud voice. "I don't recall which floor my friends were going to, and if I left the elevator I might miss them."

"That's telling 'em," thought Beth. "Just stay on the elevator, Mrs. Fillipelli—or else we die."

"You'll have to get off," repeated the operator.

"Try and make me," responded Mrs. Fillipelli,

**86**

knowing full well it would take a hydraulic lift to move a three-hundred-pounder like her.

"Stand your ground, Mrs. Fillipelli," said Beth to herself.

"Listen, ma'am," tried the operator, "I'll just go up to the nineteenth floor, drop off these three passengers, and come right down for you. If your friends get on on the nineteenth floor, you'll see them when I come back down. There's no way you could miss them."

"Well . . ." said Mrs. Fillipelli, wavering slightly.

"Don't get off!" cried Beth behind her gag, as she and Leo did their best to pound with their bodies against the top of the elevator. But no one seemed to hear us—or else they just thought the elevator itself was making the noises.

"Please," the operator pleaded. "Please get off. If the owner of the building found out I'd exceeded the elevator's weight limit in the first place, I could lose my job. You don't want to get me in trouble, do you?"

"Of course not," Mrs. Fillipelli replied. "I'll just get off here so you can go up to the nineteenth floor."

"Don't!" we called—but no one heard.

We could tell the moment Mrs. Fillipelli left the elevator—it jerked upward a good inch or two. "This is it," Beth thought desperately. "We're going to die."

"Okay—here we go!" the operator announced. "Nineteen—here we come!"

Below us the elevator's doors slowly shut; then, suddenly, we heard a loud bellow:

87

"Hold your horses! No one's going anywhere! There's something weird going on around here!"

It was Mrs. Fillipelli—mad as a hornet about something.

"It's her again," moaned a passenger.

"She's stuck her leg in so the door can't shut!" cried another.

Knowing each of Mrs. Fillipelli's legs was about the size of a full-grown sequoia's trunk, we figured our lives were spared for a bit longer.

"C'mon, lady," begged the operator. "I said I'd come back for you. So what's the problem?"

"Cookies!" announced Mrs. Fillipelli in a loud voice. "I smell cookies!"

"We're stuck in an elevator and she wants cookies?" mocked a passenger. "No wonder she's so—"

"They're my cookies!" interrupted Mrs. Fillipelli.

"What the—" someone began.

"She hasn't just lost her cookies," joked someone else, "I'd say she's lost her marbles!"

We then heard Mrs. Fillipelli grunt and figured she'd forced the elevator doors wide open—she really was as strong as she was large. When the elevator dipped an inch we knew Mrs. Fillipelli had reboarded.

Over curses and protests from the other passengers, Mrs. Fillipelli announced, "I'd know the scent of my homemade chocolate chip cookies anywhere! They are a taste sensation! And I smell them directly above us! What, I want to know, are my cookies doing on top of this elevator? I fear perhaps something has happened to the children I gave them to!"

Up in the darkness, in the elevator shaft, we suddenly remembered we still had the cookies Mrs. Fillipelli had given us.

"Listen," begged the operator, "as soon as I drop off these passengers, we'll check on top of the elevator for your cookies."

"You'll do it now," said Mrs. Fillipelli firmly.

"I won't!" replied the operator, starting to become stubborn.

"Yeah," agreed a passenger. "Don't let that hippo tell you what to do!"

"Well," said Mrs. Fillipelli, "I'm from Sicily— and when I'm right, then I fight! If you don't check this instant on top of the elevator to find out what my cookies are doing there—why, I'll . . . I'll . . . I'll start jumping up and down as hard as I can!"

"Don't do that!" cried the alarmed operator. "That could send the elevator plunging to the basement. We'd all be killed!"

"Then start looking, and be quick about it!" commanded Mrs. Fillipelli.

We heard grumbling, then noises of annoyed agreement, and finally footsteps leaving the elevator and heading off down the hallway. The footsteps soon returned ("I bet someone went for a ladder," thought Beth) and the next thing we knew, the little trapdoor on top of the elevator jerked open and the head of the operator popped through.

"Good Lord!" he cried. "There are three kids up here!"

Back in the lobby, after our rescue, Mrs. Fillipelli gave us three thousand kisses each and made us tell our story three times in a row.

"Those monsters!" she boomed. "Wait till I find them! I'll lay them down on the ground and roll all over them. When I'm done with them, they'll be so flat they'll fit into an envelope."

"Listen," said the operator, who'd not only helped in our rescue but apologized very sweetly to Mrs. Fillipelli for doubting her word, "maybe those creeps are still in that office on the second floor. It's supposed to be vacant—they probably just sneaked in early today. Let's go check."

But Suite 2-31 was empty.

We searched it top to bottom for clues, but there were none to be found.

While we searched, Mrs. Fillipelli stood in the center of the room, sniffing the air.

"Just being in this room makes me hungry!" she announced.

"Why?" we wondered.

"It's the smell of that good Italian Romano cheese," she explained. "I bet the previous tenants here were cheese importers," she added.

"Nope," corrected the operator, "they were tax consultants."

"But I smell Romano cheese," insisted Mrs. Fillipelli. "And when I smell food—I smell food."

"You're right," said Beth. "I just remembered that when we entered the room there was a pile of sandwiches on the desk. Maybe they had cheese in them."

"That doesn't help us much," sighed Leo. "Lots of people eat cheese. This won't help us find them."

"I'm afraid you're right," agreed Mrs. Fillipelli.

"And that means one thing—we go to the police. And afterward we'll have lunch."

"Whaddaya mean you were trying to find your father a wife?" demanded the policeman at the nearest precinct. "We fight crime, we don't locate sweethearts."

Beth sighed and tried to explain it all over again, but the policeman still seemed not to understand.

"You mean you invented a woman and then she turns up missing?" he inquired, his mouth hanging open. "I don't get it."

"Not quite," interrupted Teasdale, finally recovered from his fainting spell on top of the elevator, "You see, the woman we invented happened to exist, but then she vanished into the mist! And—"

"Now I've heard everything," groaned the policeman. "Poetry yet!"

We could tell that Mrs. Fillipelli was growing bored and hungry. She walked over to a vending machine on the other side of the interrogation room where we were sitting. From her frustrated gestures, Beth guessed that Mrs. Fillipelli didn't have any change for the vending machine. As Beth tried again to explain the situation to the policeman, she noticed Mrs. Fillipelli gazing with great longing at the candy bars so tantalizingly out of reach behind the vending machine's glass. Then, her hunger apparently reaching the breaking point, Mrs. Fillipelli took a twenty-dollar bill from her pocketbook, placed it on top of the vending machine, and then proceeded to rip the machine's door right off its hinges. As she was merrily stuffing candy bars into her mouth, the officer interviewing us caught sight of what was going on.

"Leaping lizards!" he hollered, jumping to his feet. "It's a burglary—and right here in the police station!"

Before we knew it, Mrs. Fillipelli had been handcuffed and charged with burglary.

"But I was just having a snack," pleaded Mrs. Fillipelli.

"She's got a large appetite," Beth explained.

"This I can believe," mocked the policeman. "And she can tell it to the judge—when her trial comes up. Till then she can stay in jail and get used to jail food."

"But I paid for the candy bars," cried Mrs. Fillipelli. "I left a twenty on top of the machine."

"Maybe," sneered the policeman, "but who'll pay for repairing the machine?"

At this point Leo joined us, looking pleased with himself.

"It's already repaired," he told the policeman. And, looking over, we saw that Leo had put the door back on so the machine was as good as new. It's sometimes a good thing having a mechanically-minded brother.

"Well . . ." muttered the policeman.

"Set me free!" cried Mrs. Fillipelli.

"I'll have to check with my commanding officer," the policeman replied. "Stay here and don't budge."

Of course, the second he was gone we were gone too.

"Let's get out of here!" boomed Mrs. Fillipelli.

"What if they sent me to jail? I'd starve to death in a week."

With Mrs. Fillipelli leading the way, we thundered through the precinct's corridors, dashed down its stairwells, and soon were gasping on the sidewalk ten blocks away—out of breath, but free.

"What about those handcuffs?" Beth wanted to know. "How'll you get them off?"

"Easy!" smiled Mrs. Fillipelli. "Don't forget I won Sicily's Heavyweight Lady's Boxing Championship."

And saying this, Mrs. Fillipelli took a deep breath and forced her hands apart with such gusto that the chain between them snapped in two!

"But what about those iron things around your wrists?" asked Leo.

"For the moment I think they make quite attractive bracelets," giggled Mrs. Fillipelli. "And when I get home, my husband, Luigi, can saw them off. Now—let's eat!"

However, just as we were preparing to enter Mrs. Fillipelli's favorite Italian restaurant, Teasdale gave a piercing shriek.

As we wheeled around in horror, we saw him being forced to the ground and pinned there. It all happened too quickly to see who was attacking him—Fudge and friends, or maybe the policeman, mad at us for escaping. But a second glance showed it was neither; it was Miss Sinknot. With Teasdale trapped beneath one of her bony knees, she was busily spraying him with Lysol and rubbing away all the dirt she could with a rag.

We all knew who June Sinknot was—but Mrs. Fillipelli did not.

"Mama mia!" cried Mrs. Fillipelli. "It must be that lady who enticed you into that office! She'd better watch out!"

And before we could explain who June Sinknot really was, Mrs. Fillipelli had leaped into action. For someone of her size and weight, she moved with astounding speed.

The next thing we knew, Mrs. Fillipelli had wrenched Miss Sinknot to her feet and was shaking her like a doll.

"Stay away from Teasdale!" she bellowed, shaking her all the harder. Soon poor Miss Sinknot was moving backward and forward so rapidly she was just a blur.

At this instant, a large garbage truck made its way down the street. It was a hot day, and the stench emanating from it was overwhelming. The truck was open in the back, and we could see it was filled with rotten food and other disgusting things.

"Now I know what to do with trash like you!" boomed Mrs. Fillipelli. And, with Miss Sinknot crying for mercy, Mrs. Fillipelli picked her up and heaved her into the passing truck, where she disappeared with a squishing sound into the garbage.

Our last sight of Miss Sinknot, as the garbage truck slowly rounded the corner, was of the unfortunate woman slowly emerging from the pile of trash, slimy spaghetti hanging from her ears and moldy grapefruit peels and eggshells all over her hair.

She looked once in our direction, and with flies buzzing madly around her garbage-covered head, she

cried out in an anguished voice, "Clean and bright! Clean and bright!"

Once the truck—and Miss Sinknot—were out of sight, Mrs. Fillipelli clapped her large hands together in satisfaction.

"Now," she said, "let's eat!"

# Chapter Fourteen

# August 13th—
# Afternoon

"Listen," said Mrs. Fillipelli with her mouth full, "you're not going alone. And that's final! Please pass the bread."

To thank her for saving our lives, we'd invited Mrs. Fillipelli to our Uncle John's for lunch the day following our misadventure. Taking advantage of our uncle's absence, we'd prepared a stupendous—and enormous!—meal. In fact, to feed Mrs. Fillipelli properly, we'd had to spend over four months of our allowances, not to mention cooking for hours.

"Yes," continued Mrs. Fillipelli, "I like a light lunch once in a while. But, as I was saying—I'm coming along with you as bodyguard. Please pass the potato salad."

In the morning, while we'd been busy cooking, the phone had rung, and it was a second person answering our ad. Needless to say, we'd been extremely suspicious, but the woman on the other end sounded so genuine, and so nice, we'd promised to stop by her apartment at three o'clock.

"All right, all right—you can come with us," Beth finally agreed.

"Great!" Mrs. Fillipelli beamed. "Please pass the macaroni."

Marie Nolan, the woman who'd answered the ad, lived in a third-floor apartment on West 21st Street. Mrs. Fillipelli had wanted to wear boxing gloves to our meeting with Marie, but we'd dissuaded her. We thought Mrs. Fillipelli looked surprising enough without them.

Marie, in fact, did seem a bit surprised to see Mrs. Fillipelli when she opened the door of her apartment.

"Hello," she began in an uncertain voice. "But I was told on the phone to expect three children . . ." We were standing behind Mrs. Fillipelli, so Marie couldn't see us.

"We're back here!" we cried.

"I'm their bodyguard," explained Mrs. Fillipelli as Marie ushered us into the small apartment.

The apartment was neat as a pin, and so was Marie. Her blonde hair was held in place by two blue barrettes and her blue eyes seemed clear and honest. Beth estimated she was five foot eight and around thirty-five years old. So far, so good.

We found seats in her compact living room and began the interview.

"Why'd you answer the ad?" Beth wanted to know.

"Well," replied Marie, "it just caught my eye, and then, when I read it carefully, it seemed to have been written all about me."

"How about the letter 'S'?" asked Leo. "Why is that special to you?"

"It's funny," began Marie, "but so many of my favorite things begin with the letter 'S.' For example, my favorite composer is Schubert, my favorite food is shrimp, my favorite drink is sangria, I drive a Subaru, and my favorite place to vacation is Sicily."

This brightened up Mrs. Fillipelli immediately, and we finally had to interrupt Mrs. Fillipelli's long speech on the beauties of Sicily, most of them culinary, to continue with the interview.

"Okay, but why is the date August 15th special to you?" asked Beth.

"It's Rusty's birthday," Marie explained.

Rusty, it turned out, was Marie's fat orange cat, asleep in a basket in the corner. Unlike Sassafras, Marie had only one cat—but she seemed as devoted to her one as Sassafras was to her hundreds.

We stayed at Marie's for a good hour or so, and by the end we all liked her a lot. The trouble was we weren't quite sure if our dad would. When Marie was out of the room for a minute, we held a quick conference and decided to invite her for dinner that night at our uncle's to see what he thought. If he liked her too, we'd arrange for our dad to meet her.

Marie was still dying of curiosity to know what our ad was all about, and we vowed we'd explain it all to her at dinner that night.

So, after giving her our uncle's address, we headed home.

"See you tonight!" called Marie, closing the door behind us.

"I know I said I liked her," said Beth, sipping her lemonade. Once again we were in a luncheonette—

Mrs. Fillipelli had wanted a snack after our interview with Marie. "But," continued Beth, "I'm just not sure we can trust her. Maybe she's working for Fudge."

"Impossible!" boomed Mrs. Fillipelli, downing her third bagel. "She's much too bright to be hanging around with a fool like Fudge. And besides—she's been to Sicily. That means she's all right."

"I admit I liked her too," Leo told us. "But I have a different idea. You know, she certainly fits our description of Sara Sanderson, right? And she likes cats, just the way old Sassafras does, right? So I say she's really Sara Sanderson!"

"Mama mia!" exploded Mrs. Fillipelli. "He's got something there."

"But why wouldn't she tell us?" asked Beth.

"Because she wanted to meet us first, to decide if she could trust us," Leo explained. "I bet tonight at our uncle's she'll admit the whole thing. I'd say the search for Sara Sanderson is over!"

"I'm afraid I disagree," countered Teasdale. "I'd say Marie is just Marie."

"Well," said Beth. "We'll find out tonight."

But that wasn't quite the way things turned out.

# Chapter Fifteen

# August 13th—
# Late Afternoon
# (from the diary of
# Fudge Ferrara)

The Boss is real pleased with me and thinks I've
done real good. I think I've done good too. But
yesterday didn't turn out so hot. Fuzzy, Footsy, and
me put those dumb kids on top of the elevator to scare
'em a bit, but when we came back an hour later from
having a beer, they were gone. I wonder how they got
loose— we tied 'em up real tight. Maybe they're not
so dumb after all. They sure do know how to fight!
Fuzzy says that kid with the brown hair who speaks in
rhyme nearly tore all his hair out by the roots. And
that blonde girl kicked and punched liked nobody's
business.

But I guess they're not that smart after all. They
didn't even see me and Footsy following 'em this
afternoon. Maybe it was because they couldn't see
around that fat dame they had with 'em. She looked
like a runaway rhino.

Anyway, we followed 'em to this place in Chelsea—
and guess who they met there? A blue-eyed blonde

about five foot eight and around thirty-five years old. I know all this 'cause I climbed up the fire escape and looked in the window.

Boy, the Boss got excited when I phoned in my description. "You found her! You found her!" the Boss kept repeating. Anyway, now that we've found her, says the Boss, we've got to get her out of the way. That should be easy. Me, Footsy, and Fuzzy know just what to do—and where we take her, no one'll ever find her. And we've even got a way to transport her; Fuzzy borrowed a van from where he works.

I never met a rich heiress before; in fact, I've never even seen a good photo of this Sanderson dame, but the Boss gave me a real good description.

The Boss says don't waste any time about it—it's almost August 15th. I says to the Boss, "Don't worry—she'll be long gone by then."

# Chapter Sixteen

# August 14th—Morning

"I'd forget about her," our Uncle John was saying. "I doubt your dad would think much of someone who breaks a dinner date and doesn't even phone up to say she's not coming."

We'd told our uncle a bit of what we were up to—but only a bit. We'd told him we were looking for a wife for our dad, not the Sara Sanderson part.

Our uncle hadn't thought very highly of what we were doing, but then he'd smiled and said, "Well—nobody could be worse than your dad's last girlfriend."

Anyway, despite the fact we'd helped our uncle make a delicious meal and we'd cleaned up his apartment so even Miss Sinknot might have approved, Marie never showed up.

At first we were annoyed, but then we began to get worried. We phoned her apartment every twenty minutes, but no one answered the phone. Finally, by ten the next morning, we were so worried we decided to go over to Marie's to see if anything was the matter. Just in case there was trouble, we called Mrs. Fillipelli.

"I'll meet you at Marie's at eleven-fifteen," Mrs.

Fillipelli informed us. "I've just finished breakfast, so that'll give me time to have a spot of brunch, too."

Over at Marie's we knocked and knocked on her door, but no one responded.

"This doesn't look good!" Beth said ominously. "I remember Marie saying she'd be home all day today."

"I'd say this calls for action," Mrs. Fillipelli told us, shaking her large head. "Stand aside," she ordered, taking a few steps back from Marie's door.

Then Mrs. Fillipelli charged.

Moments later, the full force of her vast bulk went flying into the closed door. It didn't stay closed long; wood groaned, hinges buckled, and soon what was left of the door went flying off its hinges and fell to the floor like a shattered Popsicle stick.

We stepped into Marie's apartment and looked around.

"Christopher Columbus!" gasped Beth. "Just look at this place!"

The state of Marie's apartment would have made June Sinknot physically ill: It was in total disorder, with tables and chairs knocked over and broken dishes littering the floor. It looked as though a terrible battle had taken place.

As we feared, Marie was nowhere to be found, although we did find Rusty hiding under the sofa. After we'd fed and petted him we held a quick conference.

It didn't take us long to figure out Marie had been abducted against her will. The overturned furniture indicated some sort of struggle, and we knew she wouldn't go off and just leave Rusty.

According to Leo, this proved one thing: "Marie is really Sara Sanderson!" he exclaimed. "If she wasn't, why would they kidnap her?"

"But I thought Sara Sanderson only used pseudonyms beginning with the letter 'S,' " countered Beth.

"Maybe she got smart and decided to change her way of disguising herself," insisted Leo.

There was some logic in Leo's reasoning. We decided to search the apartment for clues that might indicate where Marie had been taken.

We found none, although Mrs. Fillipelli did locate some delicious coffee ice cream in Sara/Marie's freezer.

We decided to search the street as well. We figured if Sara/Marie had been abducted, there might have been a struggle outside the building, too.

Before leaving the apartment we carefully locked Rusty in the bedroom with some extra cat food, water, and his litter box. We were afraid that if we left him free, he could wander through the apartment's broken front door. We also figured we'd better find the building's superintendent so he could replace the missing door.

We found him just outside the building. He was sweeping the sidewalk and looked extremely grumpy.

"Goldarn those slobs!" he was saying. "As soon as I get the place spruced up, they come along and mess it up!"

"What happened, sir?" asked Beth.

The man leaned on his broom and, glad to have someone to complain to, told us the following:

"I had this place looking downright pretty, I did!

All swept up nice, and I'd even planted a row of petunias along the edge of the sidewalk. Then I come down this morning and some fool's trampled them all to smithereens. And there were scraps of paper all over the place, too—a real mess!''

The site where the petunias had once bloomed certainly showed signs of a struggle.

"That must have happened when they were forcing Sara/Marie into a car!" said Beth.

"Yeah—that could be," agreed Leo.

Teasdale and Mrs. Fillipelli meanwhile started examining the small pile of trash the super had just swept up.

"Mama mia!" bellowed Mrs. Fillipelli, pointing with one of her well-padded arms. "Just take a look at that!"

We peered at the garbage but saw nothing unusual.

Bending over, Mrs. Fillipelli extracted a brightly colored morsel of paper. "See?" she boomed. "It says Palermo Cheese Importers!"

"So?" we wondered.

"So, Palermo Cheese Importers are the sole importers of the kind of Romano cheese we smelled in that empty office."

"Those creeps!" the super interrupted.

"You know them?" we asked.

"Not personally," he replied. "But yesterday, I saw their delivery van parked here. I told the driver, some dumb-looking fool in a raincoat, that deliveries had to be made round back. He just cursed at me, and this guy with him with weird fuzzy hair threw a hunk of cheese at me! Then they drove off, but my wife says she saw them again last night, around six or so."

"Did you hear any unusual noises around that time?" demanded Beth.

"Can't say I did," replied the super. "My wife and I were watching TV at the time, and we had it up real loud."

We headed to a neighborhood luncheonette for another conference. Checking the Manhattan phonebook for the address of the Palermo Cheese Importers, we discovered they were located in an area of warehouses along the Hudson River.

"That's where they must have taken her," insisted Mrs. Fillipelli, putting down her fork for an instant. "And," she added, "if I'm wrong—why, why . . . I'll go on a diet!"

"I agree that a warehouse is a likely place to hide someone," said Beth. "Let's call the police."

But Mrs. Fillipelli refused.

"For all we know," she said, "the four of us are wanted criminals by now! They still think I'm a burglar, and they must think you kids helped me escape—that's called 'aiding and abetting a criminal,' I believe. Who knows—if we went to them, they might heave us in jail!"

"If I were in jail, my heart would fail," sighed Teasdale.

"We could phone them anonymously," suggested Leo.

"They might not believe us," argued Mrs. Fillipelli. "They might just say they did—then not do anything about it! Or even worse, the one who answered the phone might be crooked—remember that guy Joe you

**107**

told me about, the one who was so mean to you? Didn't you say you'd discovered he was no good?"

"Yeah but—"

"Yeah but nothing!" proclaimed Mrs. Fillipelli. "We'll go to the warehouse tonight—just the four of us—and rescue Sara Sanderson! Anyway," she added, a smile crossing her large face, "I'd say I'm worth my weight in policemen any day of the week."

We certainly couldn't argue with that!

# Chapter Seventeen

# August 14th—Evening

"Mama mia!" exclaimed Mrs. Fillipelli, looking all around her. "This place is almost enough to make me lose my appetite!"

On one side of us rolled the murky waters of the Hudson River, its dark waves lapping against the pier where we stood. On the other side of us was a series of low warehouses, huddled together like a clump of toadstools. A boat whistle echoed from the Hudson and then the night was still.

Although we could see the lights of New Jersey twinkling vaguely across the river like a pale reflection of the lights of Manhattan behind us, where we stood was nearly lost in darkness—the only light came from our flashlights and some dim streetlamps.

"Christopher Columbus!" commented Beth, giving Teasdale an encouraging pat as she spoke, "Let's find the right warehouse and get out of here!"

"There it is!" cried Leo, pointing toward an old sign that was creaking in the night wind.

Caught in the spotlight of four flashlights, we could read its words plainly: Palermo Cheese Importers.

"Hey!" said Beth as we approached the warehouse door, "I think I remember seeing their ads in the newspaper!"

"Me too," put in Leo. "It's their fiftieth anniversary as importers, I think. And they're putting on some kind of big celebration or something."

"Never mind that," interrupted Beth. "The door's locked. What do we do now?"

"Just step back and let me at it," chuckled Mrs. Fillipelli, as yet another door proved it was no match for our hefty friend.

Stepping through the shattered doorway, we found ourselves in the warehouse. It consisted of a long, large rectangular room. The room was filled to the ceiling with immense crates and cardboard boxes as far as the eye could see. Small alleys ran between the boxes at regular intervals, reminding us a bit of old Sartorius's house. The only noise we heard was the whirring of some large machine. "The refrigeration unit," Mrs. Fillipelli explained. "They have to keep all this cheese cool."

We began our search.

In single file we made our way down the narrow aisles, pausing only to give Mrs. Fillipelli a shove when the aisles proved too narrow to accommodate her massive bulk. Above us loomed mountains of boxes while the darting lights of our flashlights, beaming this way and that, made ominous shadows on the walls.

"Marie!" we called. "Are you here?"

A slight scratching sound coming from a large cardboard container attracted our attention.

**110**

"Maybe she's locked inside it!" suggested Beth as the scratching noises persisted.

"Oh, Marie, do not fear!" cried Teasdale, "for we are here!"

"Just stand back," Mrs. Fillipelli instructed us. "Marie," she called to the box, "if you're in there, move back! We're coming to get you out!"

Mrs. Fillipelli gave a mighty kick with one of her elephantine legs, ripping open the side of the container.

The next second we raced over to peer in, our flashlights illuminating the container's interior.

Suddenly Beth shrieked, Teasdale fell over in a faint, and Mrs. Fillipelli ran squealing down the narrow corridor, knocking over cartons of cheese in her haste.

"Wha-what is it?" gasped Leo, who, being the smallest, wasn't able to see inside the carton.

Before Beth could reply, the answer itself emerged from the container, eyes blinking against the light—rats!

As we scattered down the aisle, carrying Teasdale like a sack of potatoes, a family of angry rats poured out of the large container.

With fur quivering and yellow teeth bared, the rodents charged after us down the aisle. Their squeaks echoed in the warehouse as the scratchings of their nails on the hardwood floor indicated their progress just behind us.

Beth and Leo, dragging Teasdale between us, made it to the end of the aisle with the rats narrowing our slight lead. Looking behind her as she ran, Beth saw evil-beady yellow eyes glaring up at her, while between horrible squeaks Leo could hear the panting of the rats' rapid breathing.

Just as we turned a corner, a large form loomed up in the darkness and, giving a deafening shout, heaved something large and square right at us!

For one frightful moment we thought Fudge had shown up, but a quick flash of light showed us it was actually Mrs. Fillipelli. She'd waited for us there, and the instant we rounded the corner she had thrown the largest carton she could find just behind us, blocking the aisle.

Thrown into disarray by the sudden roadblock, the rats turned around abruptly, raced back down the aisle, and disappeared through a hole in the wall on the far side of the warehouse.

"That," announced Mrs. Fillipelli, wiping the sweat from her broad forehead, "was what I call a close one!"

When we'd got our breath back, and Teasdale had de-fainted, we resumed our search—but very carefully.

"If I so much as *hear* the sound of another rat," Mrs. Fillipelli told us, "I'm going to run right through the wall, jump in the Hudson River, and keep on swimming until I get to Sicily!"

In the panic following the rat attack, Teasdale and Leo had lost their flashlights, so we were now down to two. Mrs. Fillipelli went first, shining hers, followed by Leo and Teasdale, with Beth and her flashlight bringing up the rear.

We were inching our way along the wall in this fashion when Mrs. Fillipelli suddenly stopped dead in her tracks. She stopped so quickly that Leo went charging into her large rear end, followed in short order by Teasdale and Beth. As we were attempting to extricate ourselves from each other, Mrs. Fillipelli bellowed, "Hush! I see something!"

"What is it?" questioned Leo, peering around Mrs. Fillipelli.

"I don't know," replied Mrs. Fillipelli, "but I'd say it looks a lot like a . . . like a . . . like a . . ."

"Like a what?" Teasdale asked nervously.

Beth, now peering around the other side of Mrs. Fillipelli, saw a strange form lurking ahead, pale and tall in the distance. "I'd say," she said in a hushed tone, "it looks like a ghost!"

A small thud indicated Teasdale had once again fainted, while two beams of light examined the apparition more carefully.

It was tall and broad, at least twenty feet high and fifteen feet wide; its faint yellow color seemed to glow in the warehouse's darkness like a star on a misty night. Then, in the silence of the warehouse, the odd shape began to moan.

Involuntarily we all inched backward, dragging Teasdale with us.

The moan kept issuing from the yellow mass. Whatever it was, it didn't seem very happy.

"Mama mia!" whispered Mrs. Fillipelli. "We've stumbled into a haunted warehouse!"

"Wait a minute," said Beth as the moans continued.

"I'll wait outside," replied Mrs. Fillipelli over the low moans.

"Me too!" agreed Leo. "Exit on wheels!" he added as the moans seemed to take the form of words.

"Christopher Columbus!" laughed Beth, darting forward without warning, straight up to the ghostly shape.

**113**

"Stop!" cried Leo and Mrs. Fillipelli in unison as Beth raced forward. Going right up to the object, laughing all the while, Beth gave it a slap and then tore a small chunk off and ate it!

"It's cheese!" she explained.

Joining Beth, the three others—Teasdale had now revived—all had a good laugh. The ghost turned out to be part of the Cheese Importers' publicity campaign and was actually a large sculpture in the shape of the company's headquarters back in Palermo, Sicily.

"Mama mia," chuckled Mrs. Fillipelli; "I was so frightened I didn't even smell it was cheese!"

"Now I remember," said a relieved Leo. "I saw an ad all about it. This thing weighs one thousand pounds, twenty pounds for every year they've been in business. It's supposed to be unveiled in some fancy store some time next week."

"How'll they get it there?" wondered Beth, examining the elaborate structure with admiration.

"Oh, they'll have to use cranes and all sorts of machines," said Mrs. Fillipelli. "Even *I* couldn't budge something weighing one thousand pounds."

Just then the moans started all over again. In our relief at not finding a ghost, we'd forgotten about the moans.

"Wher—where are they coming from?" asked Teasdale, looking suddenly pale.

A quick examination by Beth and Leo revealed the sculpture was right against a wall, blocking a door whose frame was barely visible just to one side of the large cheese.

"There's a door behind there," announced Beth. "And I'd bet a dollar that—"

**114**

"Sara Sanderson's on the other side of that door!" burst out Leo.

We began shouting like lunatics, some of us screaming "Sara," others screaming "Marie."

Then, from behind the cheese, came a reply.

"Help me!" cried a female voice. "Get me out of here!"

We were just trying to see if our combined strength could budge the cheese and free the door when we heard the sound of a car pulling up on the pier in front of the warehouse.

"Perhaps they'll just go away," suggested Leo.

"Not when they see my car parked there," replied Mrs. Fillipelli. "Push harder!"

But no amount of pushing could move that mountain of cheese, and no one had thought to bring a knife with us. What we really could have used was a chain saw!

"What'll we do now?" gasped Beth as we heard footsteps approaching the far side of the warehouse. Luckily for us, rows and rows of cartons and boxes stood between where we stood and where the footsteps were coming from.

"Let's hide!" proposed Leo.

"Hey!" called a familiar voice from across the warehouse. "Look, Fuzzy—the door's been smashed open!"

"You're right," agreed Fuzzy. "But why?"

"I'd say it's those dumb kids," came the reply. "And if I'm wrong, my name's not Fudge Ferrara!"

"But what'll we do with 'em?" wondered a third voice we recognized as Footsy's.

"Easy!" Fuzzy replied. "They'll all take a swim in the Hudson River—a nice long one!"

"Gosh!" we heard Fudge murmur, "I hope they brought their swimsuits!"

"That's not the kind of swim I meant," said Fuzzy in a low voice as we heard the three men clamber through the demolished doorway.

For a moment we were frozen with fear, but then Mrs. Fillipelli gave a wide grin and whispered in our ears.

We stashed Teasdale in an empty carton so he'd be safely out of the way, and Mrs. Fillipelli hoisted Beth and Leo on top of one of the long piles of cartons.

"Make your way down to the far end," she instructed us. "Then start throwing these against the nearest wall," she added, passing us each a handful of coins. "Then come right back and we'll be ready to get out of here!"

"But how'll you rescue Sara?" we wondered.

"Just leave that up to me," vowed Mrs. Fillipelli. "Now get moving, and be careful!"

Making less noise than shadows, we inched our way along the top of the long stack of cartons. Finally we found ourselves on the far side of the warehouse, about fifteen feet from the door.

Fudge and Fuzzy were already through, but Footsy had managed to get tangled up in the wreck Mrs. Fillipelli had made of the doorway. It seemed one of his long feet had become pinched in a hole and he couldn't get it out without assistance.

Footsy's mishap had given us time to make our way across the warehouse to where they were, instead of the other way around.

Once Footsy had been liberated, we began pitching the coins against the nearest corner, one at a time.

"Hey!" Fudge shouted. "I think I heard something!"

"So did I," joined in Fuzzy as Leo threw a second coin.

Beth threw a third, and soon Footsy was agreeing with his chums.

"It's coming from over there," announced Fudge as a fourth coin landed, pointing toward the dark corner. "Those stupid kids must be hiding behind some crates. Let's get 'em!"

Leaving Fudge and friends to explore the corner, we made our way back across the warehouse and climbed carefully down the cartons until we were on solid ground again—where an amazing surprise awaited us.

The cheese sculpture had been remarkably transformed. A large tunnel, perhaps five feet in diameter, had appeared in its side.

"How on earth did Mrs. Fillipelli cut this tunnel out?" wondered Beth. "She didn't even have a knife!"

Peering into the tunnel, the answer became clear— there, inside the tunnel, lay Mrs. Fillipelli, rapidly *eating* her way through the cheese!

She had just reached the far side, uncovering the door. Freeing her arm, Mrs. Fillipelli gave a mighty punch, shattering a hole in the door. The next moment a face appeared, looking dazed and confused. It was, as we'd expected, Marie, or Sara Sanderson, if Leo's hunch was right.

"C'mon!" urged Mrs. Fillipelli, starting to reverse

**117**

her way through the cheese, "Climb through the hole and follow me!"

Soon Mrs. Fillipelli had clambered out of the tunnel she'd created, Marie close behind her.

"Why are they doing this to me?" cried Marie in horror. "I was kidnapped! Then they locked me here in this terrible place! And what's happened to my Rusty?"

Assuring Marie that Rusty was fine, we collected Teasdale from his carton and started tiptoeing our way toward the door—and freedom!

As we reached the door, we heard loud shouts from the far side of the warehouse. Fudge and his companions had just discovered that Marie was missing. Next we heard their footsteps running toward us, and above the clatter Fudge shouting, "We've gotta stop them! They have her!"

"Yeah," panted Fuzzy, "and they have a car to drive her away in!"

"They're not going nowhere!" Fudge replied, nearing the door.

Fudge was right.

Stepping out into the night, we saw Fudge had parked his car so it blocked Mrs. Fillipelli's. Hers was on the end of the pier, with Fudge's in front of it, at a slight angle so it was impossible to get around it.

"Christopher Columbus!" howled Beth. "We're trapped!"

"Not for long!" boomed Mrs. Fillipelli. "Leo!" she barked. "Put it in neutral and release the parking brake!"

Leo, who was as good with cars as he was with vending machines, leaped into Fudge's long gray Buick

**118**

and followed Mrs. Fillipelli's orders. In another second he'd leaped from the car and had joined Mrs. Fillipelli directly behind it.

"Beth! Teasdale!" Mrs. Fillipelli commanded. "Help us push!"

Pushing for all we were worth, and with Mrs. Fillipelli's strength on our side, we soon had the gray car inching slightly forward. As the five of us, including Marie, shoved mightily, the car was at last rolling forward.

With one final shove from Mrs. Fillipelli, the car's front wheels dipped over the edge of the pier—pulling the rest of the car along with it.

When Fudge and friends at last made their way out the warehouse door, they were greeted by the sight of the Buick rolling slowly off the pier and sinking like a stone into the dark dirty waters of the Hudson River!

We jumped into Mrs. Fillipelli's large and luxurious Lancia. Its powerful motor soon burst to life. Mrs. Fillipelli pressed the accelerator to the floor, and the car shot forward into the night, quickly leaving the pier, the warehouse, and Fudge, Fuzzy, and Footsy far behind us.

"Hooray!" we cheered, clapping loudly and happily. "We've completed the search for Sara Sanderson!"

"Sara Sanderson?" our rescued companion replied. "Who on earth is Sara Sanderson?"

# Chapter Eighteen

# August 15th—Morning

It was a depressing breakfast.

"Christopher Columbus!" exclaimed Beth. "We search for Sara Sanderson but all we come up with is Marie Nolan!"

"Well, at least we rescued *somebody*," countered Leo.

"I know," sighed Beth, "but it's still not fair."

"What's not fair?" Leo wondered.

"It's just not fair that today's August 15th and Sara Sanderson may be cheated out of her money. She may not even know she has to show up in the lawyer's office today to collect her thirty million dollars. And if she *does* know, one of her own relatives may stop her from collecting it!"

"Yeah," agreed Leo, "and that means each of the other Sandersons will inherit a cool ten million. And one of those three is a crook!"

"You said it," Beth continued. "Just because whoever's behind all this thought we knew more than we did, we were almost killed on top of that elevator. And just because that fool Fudge thought Marie was really Sara, she got kidnapped. It's just not right that whoever's behind all this should get ten million dollars.''

"Agreed," said Leo. "But at least we *tried* finding Sara—it's not our fault if she doesn't show."

"I don't know," began Teasdale, looking at his watch, "she might show."

"What do you mean—" started Beth when a knock sounded on our uncle's apartment door.

It turned out to be Marie Nolan, carrying a large shopping bag.

"Hello, children," she said. "Sorry I'm late."

"Late?" wondered Beth. "I didn't even know you were coming."

"Put the blame on me, it was I who invited Marie," rhymed Teasdale. He then got an inscrutable look and, shaking his dark bangs from his forehead, added, "Meet Sara Sanderson!"

"So you really are—" gasped Beth, but was soon interrupted by Teasdale.

"No—Marie *is* her real name, but playing Sara will be her game!"

Teasdale was obviously enjoying being mysterious. But Beth had glimpsed the contents of Marie's shopping bag and figured out what he was planning.

"I get it," she cried. "Sara Sanderson *will* show up at Varick's office! We're going to send Marie in disguise!"

Marie nodded enthusiastically. "Yes—that's just what Teasdale and I agreed upon when he phoned me up first thing this morning. It's the least I can do to thank you kids for rescuing me."

122

"But then will *Marie* get all the money?" wondered a still-confused Leo.

"No, no," Beth explained. "We can take the check the lawyer gives us and start a bank account in Sara's name. Then we'll keep on searching for her."

Rummaging through Marie's shopping bag, we soon had her well-disguised. An enormous floppy hat hid most of her hair, a veil we attached to the hat covered her face, and a large swirling dress obscured her body. We decided we'd better do all this since we weren't *exactly* sure what the real Sara looked like.

To perfect the disguise, Teasdale found a name tag on our uncle's desk. Sticky on one side, on the other it said, "Hello! My name is————." We filled in the name "Sara Sanderson" and stuck in on Marie's dress.

"Oh, Sara," Teasdale sighed, "My dear Miss S., you're a vision of true loveliness!"

Leo, however, had something on his mind.

"This might be dangerous," he announced. "What if whichever Sanderson is behind this shows up—"

"Sidney!" interrupted Beth.

"Sartorius!" interjected Teasdale.

"Sassafras!" insisted Leo. "Anyway, as I was saying—if Sara shows up, she might very well be in danger. Maybe Fudge and friends will be waiting for her."

"What do you suggest?" Beth wanted to know.

"Well, since Mrs. Fillipelli isn't available today, I think we should go along with Marie as bodyguards."

"But they'd recognize us," argued Beth.

"So we'll go in disguise too," responded Leo.

Leo and Beth darted out to a costume shop to get

123

some props—fake beards and moustaches, mirrored sunglasses, and just in case we *really* needed to scare anyone, some very realistic-looking toy guns. On the way back to our uncle's building, Beth noticed a men's store where someone was changing the window display, and a couple of mannequins that were being removed from the window gave her an idea. They were counter-top mannequins, the kind used for displaying gloves and jewelry, and consisted only of head and shoulders, with outstretched arms.

Promising that we'd return the mannequins later that day, Beth managed to convince the storeowner to lend them to us. She was relieved when she picked them up to discover that they were made of lightweight styrofoam.

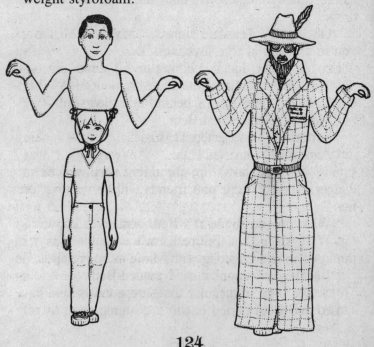

Back in our uncle's apartment, we ransacked his closet for appropriate disguises. We found a couple of old overcoats, so long that even when we held the mannequins over our heads, the coats reached all the way to the floor. We even discovered some evil-looking black hats that, combined with the stuff from the costume shop, made us look truly awful.

"I'd sure hate to meet them in a dark alley," commented Beth admiring our handiwork.

Leo then came up with a brilliant way to tie the mannequins to our heads so we could wear them like hats. It was a bit uncomfortable, but it was better than walking around with our arms above our heads, holding on.

(Teasdale has added a diagram so you can see exactly what we did.)

For a finishing touch, Teasdale uncovered two more name tags. He filled them in, removed the protective covering on the back, and pressed a name tag onto each of the mannequins' overcoats.

"Hello!" read the tags. "My name is BODYGUARD."

But while we all cheered, Teasdale began looking extremely sad.

"What about me?" he asked in a small voice.

"We didn't have any more mannequins, but our uncle did have a great tiger-skin rug, the kind with the animal's head and paws still on. Teasdale didn't think much of this costume, but we assured him that no one would blame him for killing the tiger. Once he got used to the idea, Teasdale made a very convincing tiger. He even produced a few growls that would have tricked Tarzan!

*   *   *

People stood and stared as the four of us left our uncle's building and moved toward the curb in search of a taxi. I guess we did look unusual, even for New York City. Marie, with her veil and flowing dress, resembled a princess from a hundred years ago, out for a stroll with her pet tiger. Beth and Leo looked rather odd too. With the mannequins in place above our heads, we ended up being nearly seven feet tall. We had to move slowly, not only to keep our balance, but also to see where we were going. We'd ripped small holes in our overcoats just at eye level, but they were hard to see out of. The strangest thing of all was our fake arms. Not many people walk down the street with their arms permanently raised at odd angles, and we had no way to make them move. Of course the two bodyguards' mouths were set in stupid-looking frozen smiles. Beth doesn't know who designs mannequins' faces, but she doesn't think they do a very good job.

As we stood waiting for a taxi, with Beth and Leo swaying slightly in the breeze, a crowd of curious people gathered around us. A man tried to pet Teasdale but jerked his hand back quickly when Teasdale growled. "I *knew* it was real!" he muttered. One plump woman with bleached hair was gazing at Marie with her mouth open.

"Can I have your autograph?" she begged.

Luckily, at this moment, a cab stopped and we piled in as best we could. As the cab slowly pulled out from the curb, we heard the woman's friend ask, "Who *was* that veiled woman?" to which the autograph-seeking woman replied, "It's—oh, you know who—that famous movie star who used to be married to what's-his-face . . ."

Soon the cab pulled up in front of Varick's office. We clambered out while Marie paid the driver, giving him a generous tip for any fright we might have caused him.

"I never gave a tiger a ride before," began the driver. He then gave a confused look in Leo's direction, shot a look back toward the rear seat of the cab, and then another look at Leo.

"Lady," he said to Marie. "Your friend there—is he all right?"

"Of course," replied Marie. "Why do you ask?"

" 'Cause he left his right arm in the back seat!"

"Oh, you can keep that as a tip, too," said Marie. "He's still got one arm left."

"Of all the—" muttered the cabbie. "I'm getting out of here!" he added, flooring the cab and disappearing into the heavy flow of downtown traffic.

Leo, watching the cab drive off, was upset over the loss of his mannequin's arm, but Beth was soon able to console him.

"Don't worry, Leo—with only one arm, you *really* look like a gangster! Now—let's go find Varick!"

# Chapter Nineteen

# August 15th— Late Morning

A quick look at the building index directed us to Varick's office. Soon we were stepping off the elevator on the thirty-second floor and making our way to Suite 32-F.

A well-coiffed secretary stared at us with surprise when we entered.

"May I help you?" she asked, still staring.

"Of course," replied Beth, trying to sound grown up. We'd decided Beth was to be the group's spokesperson. We'd also decided Marie was to speak as little as possible, in case Varick knew the real Sara's voice well enough to recognize an impostor. "Yes," continued Beth, "this is Miss Sara Sanderson and her pet tiger and we are her bodyguards. We're here to see Mr. Reginald Varick."

"Oh, Miss Sanderson," the secretary said, turning to Marie. "I didn't recognize you after all these years—and behind that veil, too!"

"Yes," answered Beth, still speaking for Marie. "Miss Sanderson is anxious to avoid sunburn. She hears it wrinkles the skin. This is why she always wears a veil, to protect her complexion."

"Can't she speak for herself?" the secretary demanded.

"Um," said Beth. "I'm afraid Miss Sanderson spent so much time staying out of the sun that she caught a terrible cold which turned into laryngitis."

"I see," said the staring secretary. "I'll tell Mr. Varick that you're here."

Instead of using the intercom, the secretary raced into Mr. Varick's private office. We immediately switched on the intercom to hear their conversation.

"She's here!" cried the secretary.

"Who's here?" Varick asked.

"Sara Sanderson!" replied the secretary in a breathless voice.

"What!" gasped the lawyer. "How the—" he began, then calmed down enough to ask, "Are you sure it's she?"

"I think so—I mean she's around five-eight and has blonde hair and she seems as nutty as everyone else in that family!"

"Hmmm," Varick calculated. "This could ruin everything."

"What's he talking about?" whispered Beth, but Varick's next remark clarified everything.

"Yes," continued Varick, "I'd be disbarred if it ever got out that I gave Sara Sanderson the wrong date. Sanderson said it would be worth a lot of money to us! But if Sara's shown up, I won't get a dime. I'll just have to get Sanderson to send those goons over. All we have to do is keep her here until then."

"B-but she's brought a tiger with her!" stammered the secretary.

"She always did like animals, just like that old aunt of hers," muttered Varick. "But I bet it's tame—no one walks around with a wild tiger in the middle of New York City."

"But she's brought bodyguards too!" blurted out the secretary.

"How many?" asked Varick sharply.

"Two," she replied, becoming hysterical. "And they both look like desperate characters. One's even missing an arm! And they've got terrible black beards and those sunglasses that are just mirrors so you can't even see their eyes! And they're at least seven feet tall and they never show the slightest expression. They didn't even seem to breathe. I think they must be professional killers!"

"Calm yourself, Bambi," Varick commanded. "We'll be all right—just remember how much money this is worth."

"Ooh, that two-timing crook," muttered Leo in the waiting room. "Just wait till I get my hands on him!"

"You mean your *hand*," Beth reminded him. "Remember—you left one of your arms in the taxi."

We decided it was a good time to make our entrance. Halting just inside the door to Varick's office, we paused to dim the lights so Varick wouldn't be able to see us too clearly. We then confronted Varick and Bambi.

Varick was slim and elegant but with a slightly sinister face. His black hair was brushed back from his pale forehead. With his black suit and pointy shoes, Beth thought he looked like a mortician.

"Miss Sanderson is here for her thirty million," stated Beth.

"Who told you you had to show up today?" demanded Varick angrily.

"None of your business, you crook," replied Beth as the four of us took a step forward. "Just hand over the money."

"Never!" cried Varick. "You'll never get that money!"

When he picked up his telephone and started dialing rapidly, we just knew he was phoning Sanderson to send over Fudge and friends. We had to stop him!

Teasdale acted first. With a loud snarl, he bounded forward and, pulling on the phone cord with his "paws," yanked it from the wall so the phone went dead.

Varick gave an enraged curse and heaved the phone across the room—right at Leo.

The phone went flying into Leo's mannequin's chest, and the force of the blow dislodged the mannequin from Leo's head. Before Leo could reach up and regain control, the mannequin went tumbling backward at a spine-breaking angle.

"Hah!" sneered Varick. "So much for bodyguard number one!"

The sneer slipped from his lips when Leo's mannequin suddenly whipped itself back upright just as though nothing had even happened to it.

"What the—" snarled Varick, but Beth interrupted him.

"There's no use fighting," she warned him. "We have been specially trained to withstand pain of any kind. Let me give you an example."

Beth then winked at Marie, who walked over to Leo and yanked off one of Leo's mannequin's fingers.

"See?" said Beth. "That didn't even hurt him."

Varick didn't look entirely convinced but Bambi was.

"Reggie!" she squealed in an ear-shattering voice. "Do what they say!" She then turned to Beth and howled, "Don't hurt me! I'll tell you everything!"

"Bambi! Shut up!" barked Varick. "This has got to be some kind of trick! I'm sure they're lyin'!"

At this moment Teasdale, who must have been daydreaming, suddenly perked up. "Lion," he said, having misunderstood Varick, "I'm not a lion, I'm a tiger!"

Varick and Bambi whipped around in the darkened office to see where this voice was coming from, which gave us time to get ready. When the two turned back and looked at us, we'd all put toy guns into our mannequins' hands, while Marie held two, one in each of her real hands.

Luckily the office was dark and the guns looked authentic.

Seeing guns pointed right at him caused Varick to lose all his nerve. "Don't shoot! Don't shoot!" he pleaded. "I'm sorry, Miss Sanderson," he added, "I'll do whatever you ask."

"Fine," said Beth. She plugged the phone back into the wall and handed it to Bambi, reaching out from under her coat and using one of her real arms.

"Oh my stars!" cried Bambi. "You've got three arms!"

"That's right," Beth replied. "I'm heavily armed.

**134**

Now," she continued, "I want you to phone whoever's behind this and tell him to get here on the double."

"Or her," interjected Leo.

"Then, we call the police," Beth finished.

# Chapter Twenty

# August 15th— Afternoon

It was hard waiting, knowing that whoever came through the door next was the one behind all the crimes that had been going on.

"It's going to be Sidney," whispered Beth.

"I say Sassafras," put in Leo, his gun still trained on Varick and Bambi.

"And I say it's Sartorius—" began Teasdale when the office door flew open—and in burst someone in a real hurry.

"Mrs. Fillipelli!" we gasped.

For there, in Varick's doorway, stood our friend, breathless with excitement.

"What are you doing here?" we cried.

Mrs. Fillipelli glared at us.

"Where," she asked, "are Beth, Teasdale, and Leo Smith?"

Beneath our disguises we giggled—even Mrs. Fillipelli hadn't recognized us!

"I came to make sure they were all right," she continued. "Now where are they?"

Beth quickly whispered the truth in Mrs. Fillipelli's ear.

"Mama mia!" she boomed when Beth finished explaining.

We settled back and waited to see which Sanderson would show up—Sidney, Sartorius, or Sassafras.

Soon we heard the front door of the office opening and then footsteps crossed Bambi's office, and, at last, the door to Varick's office slowly began to open.

"This had better be good, Varick," a voice muttered. "You know I shouldn't be seen too much with you."

But before the door could open all the way, Varick suddenly shouted, "Run! It's a trap!"

Before we could see which Sanderson it was, we heard footsteps fleeing. We headed as quickly as we could toward the door, but it was difficult moving speedily in our disguises.

Mrs. Fillipelli, however, was not so encumbered. "Stand back, you crook!" she bellowed, charging like a bull. She was moving so quickly there wasn't even time to stop and open Varick's door—instead she just barreled into it!

Varick's door, it seemed, was stronger than the other doors we'd seen Mrs. Fillipelli conquer. Made of good thick oak, it appeared strong enough to withstand her bulk. Luckily, though, the hinges attaching it to its frame were not as well-made. These groaned with the strain, and in a split second the door gave way from its hinges, so Mrs. Fillipelli went flying to the ground on *top* of the falling door. With a shriek and an earthquakelike thud, the door and Mrs. Fillipelli fell to earth and lay there momentarily stunned.

"Oh no!" cried Leo. "Whoever it was got away!"

"Christopher Columbus!" Beth suddenly laughed. "No one got away. Look—under the door!"

The door had fallen into Bambi's office, where the villain had been standing. It had fallen so quickly and unexpectedly that there had been no time to make an escape. For there, under the door, not to mention Mrs. Fillipelli, we saw a hand sticking out and heard an agonized groaning.

Helping Mrs. Fillipelli to her feet, we then picked up the door. And there, lying on the carpet like a rag doll, lay the guilty party, the one we'd been after.

"Christopher Columbus!" gasped Beth.

"Well what do you know!" cried Leo.

"Now you can see," boasted Teasdale, "that the right one was me!"

Teasdale *had* been correct; there at our feet lay old Sartorius Sanderson!

Within minutes the police had shown up. While we gloated, Sartorius Sanderson and Reginald Varick were handcuffed and marched off to jail. Other officers were sent to arrest Fudge, Fuzzy, Footsy, Fannie, and Joe Wypikowski. Bambi, who promised to provide evidence against her employer, was ordered not to leave town.

With Mrs. Fillipelli's assistance we had just clambered out of our disguises when a furious pounding began on the office door.

"Open up in there!" called an emotion-ridden voice.

We opened the door from the hallway—and in dashed Sassafras.

139

"Whatever is going on here?" she demanded, looking around her at all the debris in Varick's office.

When we'd told her, she heaved a sigh of relief, and putting her fingers to her lips, gave a loud piercing whistle. Moments later Olga, Sassafras's silent Russian maid, entered the office.

"Everything's been taken care of, my dear," Sassafras told her.

"Well," said Olga, "in that case—"

As she spoke, she took off her large old coat and odd cap, and there before us stood an attractive woman—blonde, blue-eyed, five foot eight, around thirty-five years old.

"Christopher Columbus!" cheered Beth. "It's Sara Sanderson!"

"Yes," smiled Sassafras. "It *is* Sara. You see, old Sigmund Sanderson told Sara all about the will a few months before he died. When Varick gave Sara a different date for collecting her inheritance, she knew that he and Sartorius were plotting together to cheat her, so she disappeared. Hah! Sartorius must have thought that he was the only one who knew the provisions of the will. But *I* knew, and so did Sidney . . ."

"Sidney!" interrupted Beth. "I thought he was behind all this."

"Not in the slightest," sniffed Sassafras. "In fact, Sidney was so concerned Sara might be cheated out of her inheritance that he put out a missing person report on her. Of course, Sartorius did too—but *he* wasn't trying to help her. *He* was hoping to find her and stop her from showing up here today, in case she

**140**

somehow found out about the will's real provisions. I put in a report, too, because I was afraid someone would think I knew where she was. I've kept Sara hidden in my home for the past year, after she'd tired of living on the run for two years. Such a good thing she likes cats and birds! We had to keep her safe, because we knew Sartorius would stop at nothing to get his filthy hands on all that money."

We told Sassafras and Sara everything we'd been through. They could hardly believe their ears, and thanked us repeatedly for what we'd done.

"So that's why you came to see me, with that silly story about library books," laughed Sassafras. "At the time I was scared that Sartorius had sent you." Sassafras then gave a sigh and continued, "Merciful heavens! People do turn into vicious beasts when they smell the scent of money!"

"Speaking of money," Sara Sanderson said, turning to her aunt, "there's something I want to tell you."

"What is it, dear?" asked Sassafras.

"Well," Sara replied. "I've seen exactly what having so much money can do to people—and I don't like it. Since I already have enough money of my own, I've decided to give Uncle Sigmund's thirty million dollars to a worthy cause."

"How laudatory!" beamed Sassafras. "I've always maintained there is nothing like charity."

"And I say charity begins at home," added Sara." I've already put a down payment on a lovely old farmhouse with lots of land around it up in Vermont— and in *your* name. I want to make your dream come

**141**

true—a home for aged and unwanted animals. And enough money to feed and care for them, too. You see, I've already signed papers that turn over the entire thirty million dollars to you as soon as I get it!''

"Oh, Sara!" said Sassafras, starting to cry.

## Chapter Twenty-One

# August 15th—Evening

Beside herself with happiness—not to mention pride in her part in solving this case—Mrs. Fillipelli decided to throw a massive party for everybody involved.

We volunteered our uncle's apartment and rushed home to decorate the place. The last balloon had just been inflated and the last streamer hung when Mrs. Fillipelli showed up with her Lancia filled to the roof with Italian delicacies. We even got to meet her husband, Luigi—the thinnest little man we'd ever set eyes on!

At eight o'clock sharp the guests started arriving—Sassafras and Sara showed up first, followed by Sidney, who brought bouquets of roses for everybody. Teasdale vowed he'd save his forever (he loves flowers) but not Mrs. Fillipelli—in the excitement of the moment she ate hers!

Marie showed up next. She brought her cat, Rusty, all dressed up in his favorite party hat—so Sassafras had someone special to talk to!

Mrs. Fillipelli had invited the elevator operator who had helped rescue us, and it was fun to see him again—on solid earth, that is.

At eight-thirty there was a knock on the door and Beth noticed Sidney Sanderson looking especially pleased about something.

Opening the door, we saw Bridget O'Sheehan, just returned from Ireland. It turned out that it had been Sidney who'd sent her the tickets; it seemed he was concerned for her safety and wanted to get her out of New York.

Seeing Sara, Bridget flew across the room and into her arms, the two dissolving into tears.

Around eight forty-five Uncle John showed up. He was a bit surprised to find a party in full swing going on in his apartment, but by this time he was used to the weird things we do!

At nine o'clock, Beth went to sit by the window to get a little fresh air. Looking down to the street below, she saw a cab pull up—and out of it stepped our dad.

"Christopher Columbus!" groaned Beth. "We forgot all about our dad's birthday! Boy—are his feelings going to be hurt!"

"Listen to me," Teasdale said, "and you'll find you're wrong as wrong can be! Filly," he called, "it's time!"

In her big booming voice, Mrs. Fillipelli commanded all the guests to be silent. She and Teasdale then lit all forty-two candles on the birthday cake Teasdale had asked Mrs. Fillipelli to bake.

When our dad stepped into Uncle John's apartment, at first he was greeted by darkness and silence—then, suddenly, on came the lights, out came the cake, and the whole happy crowd burst into a spirited rendition of "Happy Birthday to You."

"Oh, kids," said our dad in a choked-up voice, "I haven't had a surprise party since before your mother died!"

And it was a great party! Even if we didn't give our dad a wife, it looked as though we might be giving him a sister-in-law. From the way his brother John and Marie were acting, we could tell they really liked each other. We also gave our dad some important new clients: The entire Sanderson clan (minus the jailed Sartorius, of course!) decided on the spot to hire our dad to be their lawyer, now they'd discovered theirs was a crook.

We were very interested to see what our dad would think of Sara Sanderson. After all, we'd gone to a lot of trouble to find her, and she *did* resemble our dad's description of the perfect wife. They seemed friendly enough, but nothing more.

It was probably just as well. It turned out that Sara was planning to join Sassafras in the old farmhouse she'd bought in Vermont, which she wanted to make a foster home for children as well as animals. We figured homeless children needed a nice place to go more than we needed a new mother.

Anyway, after our dad had blown out the candles on the delicious cake Mrs. Fillipelli had concocted, he wanted to make a speech.

"Forget the speech!" boomed Mrs. Fillipelli. "Let's eat!"

145

Bridget    Teasdale    Leo   Beth    FILLY

Marie              John Smith

photo by our Dad

# A CAST OF CHARACTERS
# TO DELIGHT THE HEARTS
# OF READERS!

**BUNNICULA**                                              51094-4/$2.75
**James and Deborah Howe, illustrated by Alan Daniel**
The now-famous story of the vampire bunny, this ALA
Notable Book begins the light-hearted story of the small
rabbit the Monroe family find in a shoebox at a Dracula
film. He looks like any ordinary bunny to Harold the dog.
But Chester, a well-read and observant cat, is suspicious
of the newcomer, whose teeth strangely resemble
fangs...

**HOWLIDAY INN**                                          69294-5/$2.75
**James Howe, illustrated by Lynn Munsinger**
"Another hit for the author of BUNNICULA!"
                                              *School Library Journal*
The continued "tail" of Chester the cat and Harold the
dog as they spend their summer vacation at the foreboding
Chateau Bow-Wow, a kennel run by a mad scientist!

**THE CELERY STALKS AT MIDNIGHT**          69054-3/$2.50
**James Howe, illustrated by Leslie Morrill**
Bunnicula is back and on the loose in this third hilarious
novel featuring Chester the cat, Harold the dog, and the
famous vampire bunny. This time Bunnicula is missing
from his cage, and Chester and Harold turn sleuth to find
him, and save the town from a stalk of bloodless celery!
"Expect surprises. Plenty of amusing things happen."
                                         *The New York Times Book Review*

**AVON** Camelot Paperbacks